SCRAP METAL SKY

SCRAP METAL SKY

Erika Brumett

SHAPE ❧ NATURE PRESS
GREENFIELD, MA

10 9 8 7 6 5 4 3 2 1

Shape&Nature Press
Greenfield, MA 01301
www.shapeandnature.com

Library of Congress Control Number: 2015960212

For Kelly, & all he loved.

LUX

*b*ees appreciate beauty

Lux thought, or rather, Lux knew. In the hollow below his sternum. A tulip blew red and sideways. Lux could see deep down into it, where the bud hid and hunted at the same time. Where black velvet tendrils vibrated. These, his plant book labeled *stamens*. Wind riffled Lux's whiskers, bristling coarse hairs, lifting then flattening them in the same direction as the grass.

Throughout the valley of Cody County, seasons shifted suddenly, uncertainly. Spring teased with green and blooms, perfuming breezes for a week or two, only to turn on its heels and leave. Frost thawed in rivulets, only to refreeze the following evening. Clouds parted, then swept closed again like curtains.

But on this April afternoon, on his hammock swing-swaying, Lux cared only for the moment unfolding. What mattered was the now: pines spiring skyward, sunshine igniting engine parts, dew drying on dandelions. Around Lux, the junkyard was washed in white light. It glinted off metal angles and jagged edges. He shook a Bic by his ear, flicked it to flame, and lifted the pipe for a toke. Reefer smoke ovaled, hovered lenticular overhead. The sun was an unbroken yoke. Lux was stoned, content.

Beyond the eight-acre lot was an interstate. Past piles of tires, carcasses of cars, heaps of debris, was a highway. A road running straight-laned and narrow, north to south. A line of asphalt that cut black and even through farmland. He rocked the hammock. He sucked the pipe. Three bees circled.

they like what I like

Lux watched them bumblefuck the tulip, spreading petals to a pout. They loved it drunk, drunk it deep, then buzzed off. Dizzy with what they came for.

Above the bees, he swung and swatted. Lux's ass hung inches off the ground, sagging the netting to a V. Where his shirt rode up and his Levi's rode down, weed tips tickled. Imagining himself a plump fly snared in silk, Lux felt the resignation that comforts all creatures stuck. It was good to stop trying.

Spring hummed from the grass while his pipe snapped and sighed. The stem was smooth wood, the bowl knobbed—a corncob. It had once belonged to Lux's father, who would pack the chamber with tobacco, chew the bit with a scowl, clutch the shank with knuckles burled and gnarled as bark.

Between pointer finger and thumb, Lux took the tick-tock of his pulse. He pictured the stretch of artery, the delicate capillaries. Marijuana often sparked hypochondria. A certainty that, at any second, his limbs would give, his organs quit. This possibility was as probable as it was paranoid.

Just last week, he rolled a joint among branches and catkins, only to find himself stuck—certain he'd had a stroke.

Lux lost the bloodthrum of his heart, repositioned his hand. Wrist pinched, jaw clenched, he counted thuds. Thirty seconds, fifty thumps against his thumb. Over average, below fatal.

good chance I'll greet tomorrow

Feet beneath him, bulbs split paper skins, bursting shoots. Grubs munched tuber roots while, overhead, swallows swooped and wailed. A mile off, the lake glistened. Somewhere in the junkyard, his kid was playing—stacking spare parts, or making a pirate ship from sheet metal. Three days before, Lux found her asleep in a rusted refrigerator. Snoring softly, sheltered from pelting rain. He'd let her rest there, but left the door cracked so air could circulate. So he could sit down on wet ground and watch her breathe. Her entire body fit on the center shelf like yesterday's leftovers. Sadie was that small. Lux watched her 'til she woke. His love was that big.

The tulip hung its head now, stalk bent. A bee had kamikazied the flower's center, tipping ruby petals to the earth. On afternoons such as these—when hours slowed and warmth was a weight on his skin—Lux thought of Cal. Three years dead and not a minute forgotten. The musk and lilac scent of her neck, the scrape of her laugh, the ghost of her smile in Sadie's every smirk. Lux closed his eyes. He saw Calista on the windowsill, sitting prim in knee-highs, giggling. Calista on the lakeline, shivering and afraid to wade in. Calista on crank, naked on bathroom tile and marbling blue.

All along the property line, lindens waved new leaves. Winter seemed bored with Cody County, eager to go. Through a lattice of branches, Lux could see the curvature of the earth, where the horizon paled indigo into white. Biting at the pipe, he inhaled, brimmed his lungs. In the bowl, a seed exploded, making a *pop-pop*. A scorched odor rose. Lux lifted one boot (steel-toed, size 14) and crossed it over the other. They were twine-laced. Knotted, not bowed.

A painted arrow pointed at him, on Highway 5, on a sign that said:

thrift store, scrap-yard
a houseful of anything & everything

Below this—as if in afterthought—quick script scribbled:

For a cab call
332-6826

Lux coughed a cloud. It billowed from his lips, broke into cirrus wisps. Sadie always saw creatures in his smoke, pictures when he toked: a cat that arched then curled, a wisp of feather, a dragon rising. Lux just saw smoke. He coughed again, echoing a rib-cracking hack across the lot. Weed hit hardest in the morning. It tufted, wafted up and up, silver-blue, to become sky.

From behind a broken lawnmower, Sadie came skipping, hooting high and off pitch. The warble was nasal, a new habit which made Lux wince—though it would have to do 'til the girl learned to whistle. Her legs were milk-pale, her arms bare. She passed the hammock without look-

4

ing at Lux, then walked the length of the limousine, back and forth, forth and back, running her fingers through road dust. Lux looked at the lines her hand had made. Graffiti seemed to him a basic, human impulse.

we all gotta say, 'I was here'

Sadie disappeared around the back of the limo. Its gloss had matted to black, save for the driver's-side door, which was ripe cherry red, transplanted from a Pontiac. Scrawled in kid-print across the hood was the word TAXI. Dirt had splattered the windshield, dried in scabs on a foot-long crack in the glass. The back fender dangled loose below a trunk that had rusted shut.

Around the limo, Sadie reappeared. In its side mirror, she was trying on smiles: one straight on, sly with a bit lip, something mimicked from a magazine; another stretched thin beneath nostrils that freckled and flared. But it was the half-grin, posed to show off a two-tooth gap, she seemed to deem the most winning.

Lux, exhaling, agreed. He studied the child who studied herself.

she'll never be pretty, really—for whatever nothing that's worth

A fragility shivered in the way. A vulnerability that triggered pity before any recognition of beauty. Her thrift store shirts hung ragged and baggy to her knees, which were forever scraped from playing in scrap heaps. There was an intensity to Sadie's gaze, something unnerving in her stare.

kid's got anime-size eyes

They were metallic, wide-set and flint-chipped, enormous on her face. They were perpetually circled with purple, making her look like a prizefighter, or an orphan from *Oliver Twist*. But Sadie was, to Lux, more precious than a spring afternoon with nothing to do. Judgment of her came only from the outside in. From others. Never as an assessment of his own.

Across the grass patch, across the gravel drive, he beamed at the girl. Sadie, the pogo stick princess. Sadie, the keeper of toenail clippings, butterfly wings, secrets. Sadie, his sole reason for being. Her shoulder blades poked from a blue tube top. They were bone wings, tucked frail and almost touching. Sadie's left foot, bare and thickly calloused, lifted from the dirt to scratch her right calf. The skin pinked where her toenails clawed up and down, quick as a cat's. Squinting into the mirror, she shook back blonde. Her hair hung yarny as a ragdoll's in greasy need of shampoo. It would be sun-bleached by midsummer, the color of beach grass.

"Betcha it's bath day," called Lux from the side of his mouth without a pipe.

She tilted her face away from him, touching the mirror, tracing what reflected.

women . . . self-aware right outta the womb

"Ya know it's high time. . ." he inhaled and held it, "for a scrub, a dub . . . dub."

When Lux first saw Sadie, she was cradled in Cal's arms, staring him down like a sharp-shooter. She had words back then but refused to use them. Calista carried her everywhere. However heroin-wracked, however out of sorts, Cal always gripped the kid on the jut of her hip. Two years old, hummingbird-frail, Sadie had seemed a strange being. Impossibly tiny. Wiry and otherworldly. She clung to Cal, whimpered whenever set down. Walking into their lives, Lux felt he had stepped through some sort of barrier—thin but strong, invisible but unshakable. Like a spider's night work.

Sadie yelled across the yard, "Nobody needs a bath. Had one a few days ago . . . 'member?" The depth of her voice still surprised Lux, pushed from such a small frame. It had the gravel drawl of a lounge singer. A husky scritch-scratch that found its volume only in the lower octaves, as if she'd been bottle-fed whiskey.

wouldn't be so surprising, knowing Cal

Sadie sniffed in a stream of green phlegm sliming toward her mouth. "Anyways, the tub's full. I'm washing those Barbies and their Kens. So people'll want 'em."

goddamn if she doesn't break my heart on a daily basis

The house made a shadow that was long and mauve. Lux swung in and out—bright, shade, bright, shade. The hammock roped around the clothesline, creaking. Last night sat on his lips, the taste of some love dream since forgotten. Last week's sale items sat on his porch. Pillows, *Playboys*, highchairs, wheelchairs. Watercolor women and bad landscapes. Audio tapes, roller skates, silverware. A lizard (taxidermied to a husk), a lamp, a toaster, a foam mattress, a toupee. One crutch angled against the stairs.

Sadie was in charge of the children's display, though no children ever came. Her aesthetic manifested in heaps. In mounds of toy animals, shedding fluff around the unmown lawn—world-worn, and stuffed with god-knows-what. Tattered creatures, probably plucked by a grabber-machine. Probably factory-stitched by a kid.

Lux exhaled smoke that tasted stale. Around him, the scrap yard winked metal. A breeze brought pollen, the promise of sweetness. It lifted Sadie's bangs from her eyes. It lifted her face for a sniff at the wide sky.

She was not his, and Lux was not hers—in any sense, other than the girl's tidal pull over Lux's every last blood cell. Several of which, staring up, he could see. They swirled, on that first day of spring. Like white rafts floating through blue. Like life savers sliding off the side of the sun. These, his encyclopedia termed: *entoptic phenomena.*

who else has watched them?

Lux puffed a pot-waft and wondered. Had every man, looking into light, caught his own life force coursing? A cell dropped, over the corona, over his cornea, and onto the child. Barefoot in boy boxers, she seemed to sense this. Her tongue stuck out at the mirror, catching his gift like a snow-flake.

"You listenin' for calls, Baby?"

Without turning, she held the phone above her bob-cut, which he scissored, every three months, himself. This meant that she was always listening. This meant that rid-ing in Lux's limousine, taxiing dealers and sweethearts and drunks from one loneliness to another, was Sadie's favorite activity. She put the phone to her grin, pretending a cus-tomer was listening, make-believing the line wasn't dead. Her gray eyes held Lux, and his chest ached. Inaudible, she mock-talked.

Maybe she mouthed: "Yup, yup, we'll be there in five. Look for an old limo. Look for us—just us two, happy as housecats to be inside."

Or, maybe she said: "No, no, I only have a photo. She left a long time ago."

Sadie put her face back in the mirror. She slapped a hand over her laugh. It was a gesture Lux remembered from her mother. A sometimes lover. Someone he had never not loved. As clear as Calista's stare once said, *Come*, an acquaintance later asked, "Didn't she die?"

Something dark stuck in Lux's throat. It woke him at 3 a.m., lodged like a sentence unsaid. Survivors must swallow such guilt, a long-faced horse pill.

But Lux had no thoughts now except his shooting-star cells, his cradle-swing, and his wide-awake dream of Sadie.

SADIE

Life was clouds over the scrap yard, then sudden sun. Life was mealtime and bedtime, Spaghetti-O's and Lux in the wooden rocker reading her to sleep. Life was oneness, just the two of them. It was stability then change. Fixity then flux. It was endless and boundless and good.

Lux was ugly, and Sadie loved every leather fold of his face. "It's a sad dog face," she once told him, bouncing his jowls in both hands, puppy-licking at fat tears. Lux always cried at night. Remembering Calista kept him from sleeping, and Sadie kept him from forgetting.

"Your face makes me happy and hurty. All at the same time."

"It's yours then," he answered.

The only other thing that was Sadie's, and Sadie's alone, was her own self. Lux told her that, too, long ago.

Across the train tracks (*look both ways*). Through the acre of dandelions (*make a wish*). Past the lakefront school, past children who knew chalkboards and packed lunches, was a land. Farther than the last mailbox, beyond the pavement's end, there spread a space more angular and alive than any city. This place was shared. It belonged to them: to Sadie, to Lux, to their togetherness. A kingdom of metal and rust and cheese sandwiches melted by blowtorch.

"You like 'em brown. I know. Papa's gotcha." Lux buttered the hubcap and slapped down a slice of bread. The sun glowed low and gold over the junkyard, shafting sharp light through scrap piles. Sadie hoped, not for the first time, that "The House-Sit Bandit" wouldn't get lost in all their metal. Or distracted by all their for-sale toys.

The whole town was talking—about the break-ins, the slip-outs. About the backdoor escapes and the cops' runaround. Last week, from the cab's backseat, a customer called the intruder a "he." But Sadie knew better. "He" was surely "she," and it was only a matter of time before her mother found the right house.

Calista was the smell of menthols and oatmeal in the morning. She was the empty space inside Sadie when she lay flat on the mattress, searching for faces in ceiling cracks. Calista was a lullaby she couldn't quite recall. Calista was cool fingers across Sadie's forehead, sags around Lux's eyes. She had one clear memory of her mother: Cal sitting on a windowsill, picking scabs from her forearms and giving them to the wind. This image stayed with Sadie wherever she went. It was cropped, ragged around the edges, ripped from context. She kept it close to her, like a photograph snipped to fit a locket. Sadie knew—as well as she knew the scrap yard, the scrape of the oak's bark, the crescent-moon scar on Lux's back—that Cal had hurt them. That some gashes can't be stitched shut. That longing underlies everything.

A car passed on the highway. A plane passed overhead. Melted against the hubcap, the butter was nut brown. Lux sucked his pipe, hands over heat. "Looks good, huh?"

"Not the insides, though. Don't burnt the cheese brown."

He reached to touch her nose where it scrunched. "Found a new one. We could make a fortune off your freckles." Lux unwrapped a square of processed, orange cheese. When he sandwiched it, the hubcap spat grease. "Sit back from the flame a bit, Baby."

Sadie leaned in. "I love the first sniff you get when it's cooking like that."

"Take a seat. Then tell me how old you are." The seat was a milk crate. It stayed vacant against gravel. Sadie pulled at a sock. No matter how she tugged, the left one always sagged.

"Let's eat two each again." She wiggled her tongue through a space in her smile. A few days ago, Lux had dental-flossed the tooth to a doorknob while Sadie breathed, *hurry up*, out of an open mouth.

"How old?" His voice was rough, gruff around the vowels. This happened when Lux was fed up. Which was just another way of saying he was hungry.

She answered, "Four," as practiced over every meal, for the past two years. It was the age Lux made her stay.

He nodded, stubble-shaking, yes. This meant, *good, good girl.*

Sweat slid down his nose, pooled, then dropped. It hit hot metal with a sizzle, and Lux said, "Salt."

"Ewww," said Sadie. She scratched at a bug bite blotching her wrist. "Wanna play our word game? You know, while we sit and wait?" Only then did she take the milk crate seat.

He cranked the torch dial to full flame. "Nah, not now, Love. Another time."

"K, I'll start."

To name was to own, so they'd made a new game—a diversion of words, their world relabled. Sadie understood, somehow beyond language, that the point of play was new language, life reinvented. Last round, under the porch and waiting out rain, she'd started with the word "knees." Lux translated, coined the term *shin hats*. Thus a crow became a *plumed ape*, his bellyrolls a *crumb bank*. Lux dubbed the ceiling fan the *deheatifier*, and Sadie *the stub pirate*. Nipples were *flesh pebbles*, and apricots, he said, were definitely *shitty peaches*.

The sandwiches crackled on the hubcap, bubbled cheese and fat. Through smoke and dusk, Sadie watched the house dance.

"So, you wanna go first? How 'bout, home. What's your new word for home?"

"Dammit, I said not now."

She stared at the torch. Lux liked to act tough, to play rough. But Sadie knew he was squishy as his belly, soft and sweet-centered as a Twinkie. Which was why, only the day before, she had redirected his gaze, distracted him from the side of the road, from the doe who lay splayed and bleeding, guts spilling out like spaghetti sauce. Lux was swerving the limo, silly-singing a song they'd made up about a customer. Sadie was laughing along, smiling out the window, when she saw the deer. The eyes were soft and wide and still blinking.

The hoof had split from its leg bone and was jutting skyward.

Without a thought, she'd pointed to the opposite side of the highway. "Is that the driveway where we dropped off that one guy? The one who's gots lots of horses?"

Lux's head turned, away from Sadie, away from the dying deer, and she knew he'd feel all the better for it. After major losses, small deaths were too much to take.

some things Lux shouldn't see

Standing in the scrap yard, slouching in sagging socks, she watched him flip their sandwiches. When he bowed to check for burn, Sadie grabbed the bread bag. Lit bright against torchlight, Lux's profile blazed. He could still be her papa, whether he knew so or not.

From a slice of white, the girl bit three dough holes: a pair of eyes, and a long, crooked mouth. The bread went back into its bag.

this is whatcha get, thought Sadie, *when I'm your girl.*

STERLING

When Sterling Tate sank to the elbow in bathwater, Ursa grinned gums. Dentures were reserved for visiting hours—even though, for Ursa Simone, visitors never came. Sucking puckered lips, she sat submerged to the navel, silver to the temple. She had a back that was broad and sun-splotched. On the third vertebrae down her spine, a mole rose, mossy-round as a river stone.

Kneeling, Sterling leaned against the tub, soaped her shoulders, sponged her clavicles, her knees, the tender dips between her toes. Ursa slapped at lather. She splashed suds, speckling the pleats of his uniform, soaking the cotton of his carefully tucked shirt.

"Hey now." Sterling gripped her wrist, hard. It was muscular, thicker and hairier than his own. Ursa's eyes rolled back. Beneath her irises were spaces, blue-sheened scleras the tint of skim milk. She had the jawline of a lumberjack, the hulk of a Mack truck. Her bangs were thinning white, bobby-pinned to one side, wisping to nothing like tufts of cotton candy. Sterling sat back on his haunches to watch her.

Beyond the walls of the facility, Cody County circled a glacial lake, looping and twisting back into itself—a colossal Möbius strip. The town had been founded for gold miners, for a forty-family community that settled above fine-grain sand, nestled below pines and gothic alpine spires. A century later, tourism took over: summer sunbathers, winter snowshoers. Wineries, casinos, motels, boat rentals. The nursing home sat on the north shore, rising four-stories above topiary, February, and a small, leaf-clogged fountain. Bright Horizons offered shore views to the older, top floor residents. Parking lot vistas to the lower-tiered, those further from rent-paying relatives and death.

In three years, Sterling had worked his way up from laundry. From washing bed sheets to washing body parts. The facility had given him CNA training, new orthopedic sneakers, justification for breathing and being. Nothing meant more to Sterling than clocking in midmorning, clipping on his nametag, moving from room to room with responsibility and routine.

Ursa rocked in gray water, agitating suds and Sterling. He closed his eyes, sighed. In a gentler timbre, a softer, bath-time tone, he asked, "Wanna wash your ears?"

"Sterling!" Her treble echoed off the tub, high-pitched off tile. He was sure her words had been locked away all week, saved for this day—the Scrub-n-Shove shift—as dubbed by employees on its assembly line. Sunday, at Bright Horizons Care Center, meant lukewarm water and Hoyer lifts, luffa bars and employees with sore backs. Around the massive island that was Ursa's torso, Sterling steered soap.

He lathered, up and down, to and fro over loose flesh. Waves lapped at liver spots. Lilac steamed with Ursa's yeasty smell, and Sterling knew she was remembering.

Past the whitewashed stall, the porcelain station where he scrubbed, a resident was screaming about heaven and Betsy. About a doll left on a train. But if Ursa heard, she showed no sign. Steam rose, while Sterling washed with a low hum, with warm rinses down her spine. In the hallway, the cries continued.

"Stop the engine! Oh, my doll, I forgot my GOD-DAMN DOLL!" There was shuffling outside the door, heels dragging rubber.

Sterling watched a bubble bulge under Ursa's chin. It speared on stubble and popped.

In the corridor, the woman howled, "My dolly's on that train. What don't you understand? My dolly!"

Then all was quiet but the *plink* of the faucet. It trickled at irregular intervals: *plop-plip, plash-plish.* Ursa lifted a hammertoe from the suds to plug the spigot. Soaping the knots in her neck, the hump on her back, Sterling imagined Ursa's body as it once had been. As it was before years creased wrinkles, before decades varicosed veins. Surely she was youthful, though never fragile. Full, though never feminine. Beneath his fingers, Sterling felt sinew and latent animal strength. He felt power. Her lashes fluttered, short and colorless, against crow's feet. His nametag clicked plastic against bobby pins.

"Like the way I did your hair? That how you used to style it, once upon a time?" He maintained a voice that was level, cool. As if this were any other day. As if this day were not his last.

Water sloshed in a small space of silence.

"Time upon a once," she said, fingering upswept strands. A wisp of gray frayed out, stood on end. Sterling retucked it as he tested the bath temperature, added a splash of hot. Ursa's eyes met his.

The bar of soap slipped from Sterling's grip to skid the ridges of her spine. He reached deep to retrieve it, while Ursa rocked ripples into water. Hanging from her limbs was muscle grown old, tendons sagging wrinkles—skin which once stretched over ligaments, corded and hard, without a trace of fat.

"Feel good?"

"Tate is leaving. Sterling Tate," she answered.

circular scrubs, lift one flat breast, then the other

Ursa yanked at his nametag, and Sterling yelped.

Even on days off, he wore it. Pinned to his Polo in the Thrifty-Mart, glossy against boxers in the blank dawn. It was Sterling's tag—his badge, with his title, and Windex polished it well. Vaseline kept the clasping smooth. Puckered in the right-hand corner, pixilated to a square inch, was his face: stunned yellow by flashbulb, startled by bright. A thicket of flesh-colored hair blended into his cheeks, which blended into the picture's beige background. He often felt the gaze of children fix there—on his tag—rather than following the path of greatest resistance, up his neck, to the pale of his stare. Waiters often mistook the photo for a smear of tartar sauce, for a clod of cold gristle, and he accepted their extra napkins with a nod. Sterling attached the label, nightly, to his pillow. In the dark, he touched it. Lips opening around words his fingers covered like Braille:

STERLING TATE
Bright Horizons Care Center
Certified Nursing Assistant

"Tate! Tate!" Ursa bellowed, pulling the nametag, and Sterling, closer to her bathwater, to her big thighs, where he saw bubbles and leg hairs magnified. This was not to be rough, he understood, just to remind. Most staff members still didn't believe in the strength of Ursa Simone. Despite her windowsill display of 1950's trophies (an army of pedestaled muscle women, miniature biceps raised in bronze). Despite her handprints (left, like breath on a window, across Sterling's neck). Despite her roommate (who woke up dead in a rolling bed outside the cafeteria). But it was not to be rough, he understood. It was just to remind.

"Wash 'em, behind 'em."

"Okay, all right." He unclenched Ursa's hand, meaty and square-nailed as a man's, from his nametag. A bobby pin swung loose on a white strand. Sterling replaced it on top of her head, where Ursa's scalp peeked through in patches.

"Ears!" she grunted.

"Yes. I know." It was typically at this point in Sunday's shift when calm washed down the drain, when he fought to leave Ursa for sixteen other South Wing residents, all of whom were to be bathed by noon.

"Back scratches."

"Nope. Only twenty minutes 'til Group. Let's get you out." Sterling's image of "Group" was vague and indistinct. Wandering past the Activities Center, he'd noted a tiny, hoop-earringed therapist who spoke too loudly, a CD of whale calls played on loop, and a liberal use of finger paint. What Ursa did during these sessions was beyond Sterling's imagining. He washed the angles her shoulder blades made, sudsing them longer than he normally would have. Ursa swashed a great wave drainward.

"'Bout ready, huh?" he said, standing. "Ready to dry off?"

"Bye, bye. See ya later, soon." Her voice came harsh, husked. One enormous ear, curved as a conch, leaned into Sterling. He pulled back, but its wet print stayed pressed to his uniform.

"Gotta call for a lift . . . unless you're gonna help today?"

Ursa paused. "Hoyer. Hoyer-lift."

yeah right, you could lift the entire thing with me in it

Sterling shook his head. He knew she was capable. Of washing herself, of feeding herself, of flexing her secret strength to great consequence. As when, for instance, the mailman swore he saw Ursa on the roof. Or, as when she reportedly tossed Crawford—room #8, East Wing—over the back of his oxygen tank. (The only witness said that his broken rib didn't hurt much, that he was forever grateful to Ursa for saving his life, and that the tater-tot flew at least four feet from his throat.)

Or as when she was allegedly asleep, last Sunday.

That's what the police report stated—Ursa Simone was sleeping. But Sterling knew better. He'd been restocking rubber gloves when she passed at the end of the hall. Padding down dawn-lit tiles, pushing a bed. A bed with a squealing left wheel, a crib of safety bars, and a dead roommate tucked in snug. But Wren was not dead then. At least, not yet. Just dreaming, and snoring way too loudly for Ursa, who had decided to relocate her. Wren would not be dead 'til she sat up beside the cold-cuts counter of the cafeteria. 'Til her frail frame expired from shock, and Sterling tried to shake it back to life.

In the tub, Ursa's squint cinched with concentration. "Stack 'em up," she said, grabbing the soap from Sterling's hand.

"Oh, no. Hey now. No stacking today, come on." Sterling snatched the bar back, just as she had its slick underbelly balanced on the shampoo bottle, which was on the conditioner, which teetered on the pumice stone.

"Uuhhh, build 'em high," she moaned, as the items toppled, splashed.

In three years of employment at Bright Horizons, Sterling had watched Ursa stack everything from saltshakers, to catheters, to dried cockroaches from the corner. She piled diuretic pills on remote controls, on lumbar pillows. Vases on bedpans, on pyramided clipboards. Stacking was her diversion, her relaxation, her obsession. There was no end to the joy Ursa Simone experienced with new objects placed one on top of another.

The strange, wobbling piles reminded Sterling of trailside cairns. Mysterious monuments—unsteady, unsettling—someone saying in stones, *I was here*. He had always wondered (when bending in his hiking boots, when frowning in his uniform) if the stacks were directional markers. If they indicated a memorial, a final resting place. Or, if they were arbitrary pilings whose sole significance was that they had none at all.

"Stack 'em up," she moaned.

"Nuh-uh, let's get you toweled."

Limp, and suddenly without strength, Ursa reclined against the tub.

"Aw, come on, Ursa, of all days to act like this." How much she understood of his "dishonorable discharge" Sterling was unsure. Coroners had deemed Wren's death a result of cardiac arrest, of natural causes, which—along with security cameras—absolved Sterling of blame. But the family's attorney kept calling with more and more questions for Bright Horizons. How was Wren out of her bedroom, but still in bed? What septuagenarian was strong enough to wheel Wren that distance? Who was on shift that Sunday morning, and why in the world would he move an old woman in her sleep? Does he have a record?

It was clear that Sterling, the only employee present, would never be believed. Legally exonerated or not, he would never be vindicated, and Ursa would flex her false fragility long after his nametag was relinquished—long after his identity was returned.

Sterling pulled the tub plug, heard a sucking as the drain swallowed. Ursa abandoned her stacking and sighed.

Any account of her abilities, like her history, depended on who was in the staffroom. Francis—the second-floor receptionist—told Sterling that, before suffering a severe stroke, Ursa had been a six-time Olympic wrestler, a Russian one. Tony from laundry heard that, before a horrific juggling accident, she had been a child circus sensation, a bearded one. A security guard started the rumor that, before WWII, she had been a man, a brave one. But most employees, on most rotations, recognized Ursa only by her patient ID: #1173. And by her startling stature: at once solid and stooping.

On different shifts, in different sections of the care center, Sterling would catch sight of Ursa. Sometimes spilling over the arm of her wheelchair to stare at a bare wall. Other times, slumped at a card table, surrounded by a dozen other residents. Or, more often than not, plodding toward lunch in her short robe and sagging skin. Sandwiched between two smaller nurses like a pot roast between croutons.

The tub gurgled, gulped, while the old woman pulled at Sterling's uniform, stretching the sleeve. "Back scratches, Ursa's back."

"No."

"Scratch, scratch, Tate," she cooed heavy, throaty. He could hear her urgency.

"No." Sterling stood. He poked his head into the hallway, dialed #59 on the wall-phone.

no way I'm rubbing your back, not today

"Sterling!"

Three back scratches later, the loudspeaker whined, "Hoyer-lift to sanitary station seven, Hoyer to seven."

Ursa tilted her head at the sound. "Cancel lift, cancel," she said, eyes rolling above Sterling's scratching, toothless grin spreading.

———

It seemed to Sterling, moving through Bright Horizons, that everyone was staring at his shirt pocket. At its square of bare fabric. A huddle of scrubs stopped talking when he walked by. A lady, shriveled and tethered to an IV pole, laughed hysterically as he passed. Two old men looked up from their laps. They squinted at Sterling's chest, and he touched the pinholes where his nametag once pierced.

A polka dot nightie hobbled toward him, stabilized by a steel walker. On the right handlebar, a cup-holder had been mounted. Her dentures were too big. Sterling accelerated toward the elevator.

Reaching out a palsied palm, she said, "It can't be that bad, Hon."

if you only knew

There were ovals of rouge on the woman's cheekbones. She was fragile, elfin, grasping at Sterling's elbow. He glanced back. Her eyebrows rose, penciled in autumn pumpkin.

Sterling's soles squeaked against linoleum. He inhaled Pine Sol and canned peas from the cafeteria. Management had informed him that his last paycheck would be mailed promptly. They said that his scrubs must be laundered and returned, that he'd be surprised what it saves them annually. Sterling considered this as he walked.

Through sliding doors was a lake and a quiet community, rain rushing gutters, and Cody County. A town with paper snowflakes still taped to school walls. A predictable town, with lawn gnomes, pedophiles, leaf piles. Heartaches and door wreaths, toothaches and potlucks. A stagnant town, all for God and football, with ass-numbing city council meetings, bake sales, and expanding cemeteries. Quaint, cookie-cutter homes with porch swings, fridge magnets, and tea cozies knit in the shapes of sheep and cows. There were Frisbees on roofs, baseballs through windows, gossip under helmets of salon hairdryers.

Out the nursing home exit was a six-block walk to a studio apartment. Inside, Sterling Tate would find the emptiness that curled up waiting for him. He would fall on a single bed, listen to the sound his sobs made pressed deep into it.

Yards away, the elevator opened, then closed. Perspiration pearled around Sterling's collar. He needed air. And dark. Moments earlier, in porcelain veneers and a suit, his boss had shut a door, making a gold plaque shake in Sterling's face:

WALT CHIPLEY
Bright Horizons Care Center
Executive Director

Standing outside the office, fired and forlorn, he'd run a finger over Chipley's name, over its little ridges of gold embossing, and tasted hate.

"Sterling? My God, there you are!"

He turned from the elevator to see Bridget, the chubbiest candy striper on shift. Reaching out, her hand grazed his arm hairs. They stood on end, as if static-charged. Sterling took a step back—any physical touch, beyond the intimacy of his job (or, what had been his job), was unbearable.

"I've been looking all over! Come'ere a sec. Hurry up." She motioned with her chins down the corridor.

"Can't."

"It's really very—"

"I'm leaving." He said it hard and flat, then pushed the

button, its down arrow already lit amber. He pressed again, harder.

"But it's Ursa—"

Sterling blinked.

"She keeps on saying, over and over—"

"Listen. My nametag, it's all turned in. I gotta—"

Bridget grabbed his hand, "'Tate.' It's all she can say, again and again: 'Tate, Tate!'"

By the time they reached room #11, a crowd had clustered in the doorjamb.

"What happened?" asked Sterling. Bridget pushed forward. The round hip of her scrubs parted wheelchairs, whispers.

"Go on. Get back to yer own beds!" she pressed through the doorway. "Sterling, come here, come."

But just two steps in, Sterling stopped. Stunned. He looked around the room where Wren once snored, the square area lined with support bars and purple-painted forget-me-nots. Dust bunnies cowered in corners.

Sterling stared, trying to make sense of the space.

Into the center of the room, Ursa's wooden dresser had been dragged. Positioned on top, emptied and overturned, was the supply shelf, upon which one bed mounted another. A recliner lounged, footrest kicked out, above the dresser, the shelf, and the twin beds. The recliner dipped where a wheelchair sat in its seat.

Sterling's breath stuck. His eyes climbed the stack, which appeared remarkably stable, structurally sound, and his chest swelled with wonder. With relief and the hope of being believed.

Grinning in the wheelchair, inches from the ceiling, Ursa topped her tower.

"Ursa was here!" she hollered down. Her eyes held Sterling's, "Strong girl!"

THEO

Parrots often outlive people. Sometimes, parents outlive children. A parent will inherit, on occasion, a parrot. Theo's swung night-watch in a cage above his bed. Her chest crested bright lemon, her back molted baby blue. Feathers fell toward the pillow. They drifted through darkness to catch in his stubble like snow.

Theo rarely answered the door, and rarely did anyone knock. Housekeeping at the Blue Moon Motel pushed soap and fresh sheets past the "Do Not Disturb" sign, past the polyester curtain, which stretched orange and olive stripes the width of his window. Maids stopped to thump short, sharp knocks, but only when Theo's towels went a week unwashed. Roadtrippers rattled the wrong key in his lock, but only when lost. Teal Ellis put small fists to his door, double *tap-tapping*, soft and urgent as her name, but only when lonely.

The sound made Theo jump, and his pen drop.

Teal

"Pretty girl!" screamed the parrot. She rocked her perch

to a pendulum, beak-bobbing at the door. "Pretty pretty!"

"Shhhh, Ferrah," shushed Theo. "Quiet!"

On the edge of the bed, on the edge of a three-day drunk, he recognized Teal's knock. And the sound of rain—pattering steady, splattering the flat roof of the motel. All of Cody was awash, a week deep in relentless wet. It was the kind of rain that soaked through wool sweaters, seeped through shoe soles. The kind of rain that flooded gutters, cancelled little-league games, made lovers lean close for cinematic kisses. It was the kind of rain Theo could lie down in.

Tremors had caused him to draw through the paper napkin, which he folded now, and slid under his pillow. He produced dozens, daily. Cocktail canvases, small sketchpads delivered with a drink. Stacks of them, and on each square: Teal's portrait, in India ink. Rimmed with red wine, and shoved behind the motel mirror to remind Theo of love.

A dull thud shook the door—Teal's elbow or stiletto.

Ferrah shrieked. She shrilled a high C, which warbled, then dipped into the two-note catcall whistled by construction workers and caged parrots alike.

"Pretty bird!" screeched Ferrah, as Theo threw a wine cork at her bars.

Cody County had become home, two decades earlier, because Theo ran out of gas above its deep lake. He was drunk-driving a '67 Dodge down the highway—swerving and sobbing toward nothing, away from everything—when water gleamed through a cleavage of hills. When he sputtered to a stop beside a sign that said: "Welcome to Cody, Home of the Trojans." In smaller print (with two letters scratched away by juvie-bound townie boys) were the words: *Please d i e slowly.*

Theo had continued toward Cody on foot, Farrah's cage swinging and singing from his outstretched arm. The lake was glassy that day. His daughter was two weeks dead.

Rolling now, from the motel mattress, Theo staggered two steps. Then sat again. He remembered the week's rent, overdue. The walls breathed with him, and the design on the carpet refused to hold its pattern. There was a rocketing in his gut, preceded by a plummeting, which made Theo reconsider the term, "center of gravity." Rain pummeled the windowpane while Ferrah flipped on her swing. She bird-purred to the *clack-clonk-clack* of the heater.

Teal rapped again. Louder.

impatient as ever

The parrot squawked, "What the fuck! Pretty girl! Fuck!"

"Just a sec," answered Theo, who was reflected—sallow, waxen, twitching in his own skin—above the television. The station had fallen off air, and vertical columns colored the screen. They cast a strange glow over the man, over Ferrah biting at her bars. A hand leapt from his lap. He finished the inadvertent jerk with intention, shaking a blue-veined wrist toward the nightstand. Three swigs of Shiraz. Theo stood. The bottle wobbled on its coaster, a Gideon's Bible that worked days as a window-prop.

"One second," he tried to stand. "Fuck."

"Pretty! Love my pretty! Fuck!" repeated Ferrah. Theo could hear Teal out in the wet, shifting high-heel to high-heel.

From the moment she moved into the Blue Moon, into the room next to his, Theo felt the need to still her. The need to freeze her frame, to pen a new portrait every time she stirred. Every time she swayed curves under a broken disco ball. He tried, nightly, but even her abdomen moved. In constant, muscular motion. It bounced a bellybutton ring, flexing and fluttering, out and in, at the audience.

Teal was swivel-hipped, hazel-eyed, and slow-blinking. There was a sleepiness to her stare. Not a lack of awareness, exactly, but a laziness—an adolescent's indolence. Someone lounged behind her lids, loafing on a daybed in house slippers, hungover beside a box of half-eaten bon-bons. While her eyes never widened all the way, her lips were always slightly parted. Like a pinup girl, or a suckerfish. With languid laughs, with lashes that batted low and bored, she seemed to say, "I'll get up when damn well ready. I have the rest of my life to start trying."

Evenings, Theo waited for stiletto-stomps past his peephole, for Ferrah to spread her wings wide with excitement. On the walk to work, sidestepping potholes and puddles, Teal pressed on longer lashes. Her makeup ran in the rain. Theo followed with the dusk. Past the bus stop, its dank musk, and the bag lady living there. Past the Jack In the Box, the ampm, the sandwich board that read: "Manicures, Pedicures, Palm Readings." Four blocks and his drink would be waiting beside a stack of napkins. Teal knew what he liked. At the club entrance, she would turn, hair raven-sleek and dripping, eyes smudged turquoise. She would scan the street for Theo, who trailed blocks behind, coughing white breath into winter like an old caboose.

His booth against the back wall was always vacant. It had a springy seat and duct tape seaming the vinyl. Legroom and a smooth Formica table. There, he sketched her features—and the spaces in between. Tremors tore through napkins as his ballpoint dreamed: Teal, turning empty-eyed to wink at a regular; Teal, drawn in fast-forward, penned at her pole, arching back brown nipples and sadness.

Theo drew her filtered through him. Through cognac, music, and cataracts, at the Ribs 'n' Racks strip club. He watched men watch Teal twirl in cigar haze. They sucked sauce from barbequed bones. They licked their fingers, then their lips. They tightfisted single bills, never turning toward one another.

"Be right there," he yelled over the parrot. Some distance beneath him, Theo's socks moved across the carpet. He swayed, as if on the deck of a ship, and the door bobbed far off, blurring the horizon line. Vaguely, indistinctly, Theo felt his bathrobe swing open, his big toe stub the bureau.

"Hold yer horses, Girlie. Shit."

"Shit. Busy busy! Go away!" squawked Ferrah. It was the tune Theo had taught her.

Through the tondo of the peephole, Teal looked barrel-distorted, convexed. Clouds swirled, rococo behind her, white against the night sky. He opened to rain and her body bent. She was righting wine bottles along the wall.

"Oh!" She stood, lengthening in latex, glass gleaming in her hand. There were raindrops gliding down the window, sequins glinting down her dress. Water fell all around, and her hair was pulled back tight against the storm. Against wind and frizz-inducing drizzle. On her crown curled a black bun, shampooed and coiled at noon, when she woke. It would be freed and teased at ten, when she worked. Her lips were chapped, cracked under slick red gloss.

Teal turned heads in the grocery store, tricks in the strip club parking lot, and would be twenty-two in the spring. She gave Theo a smile, slightly in profile, as was her style. Leaning in the doorjamb, in fake lashes and next to nothing, she looked haggard. Used up. Her left bra strap was tattered, yellowing.

ah, poor kid

He hated what she wore to work. Even more, he hated that she took it off at work. Both Theo and Teal kept a safe distance from her body. He, with a tender, fatherly discretion—with a fear that was lusty and writhing. She, with a remote restraint—with a customer's compliance to the four-foot rule.

Teal shivered. Wind covered her bare arms in bumps. Theo thought to touch them, then he did not. He thought of his little girl, long ago gone. Then he did not. The child lived now in a heart-shaped, ceramic box, in a suitcase, in the silence of his storage unit.

"Here ya go." As if offering a housewarming gift, Teal pressed the cold curve (what had been warm Chianti) into Theo's palm.

"Another dead soldier," he said, scanning the line of bottles. "Executed at dawn."

The motel's neon flashed sapphire in their glass. Raindrops gave them rhythm. She leaned forward for a half hug, tapping Theo's back with the brisk, brusque efficiency of an airport pat down. On the collar of his bathrobe, Teal left a smudge of flesh-tone foundation. When she shook dry beside the bed, his room filled with the smell of Pall Malls, bubble-gum, mildew.

"Pretty parrot," the girl said, approaching Ferrah, "yes, you are." Each cooed and clucked tongues at the other. She reached up a pinkie for the bird to gnaw. It ducked and danced around Teal's nail polish like a boxer. Ferrah flirted, blinking glass-bead eyes, puffing to twice her size.

Droplets dripped from Teal's raised elbow. Theo was watching one slide down the back of her knee, then she turned, faced him, and said, "I have something to tell you."

TEAL

Ever since that night, when streets shone silver with rain, and she stood staring too long in her motel window, wearing baby fat and panties, she knew. Ever since that 1:00 a.m., when the iron lay angry-side down to burn the Virgin Mary through her halter top, onto her ironing board, and into her dream, Teal knew she had to tell Theo. About water oil-slicking the window in sheets. About the smell like toast browning, the fire extinguisher, and the ironing board puffing smoke on its three legs. About the aura that steamed in a sepia-toned semicircle. And Mary, faint as a prayer, at its center.

Teal smiled up at the parrot.

soon, Ferrah, you'll see

Where the cage screwed into the ceiling, plaster had chunked away. Dried bird shit caked the lampshade below.

"So after Mary appeared on the ironing board, I just folded her back into my closet," she said, holding both hands over the heater. Her dress was nearly dry.

"But then, I had this amazing dream, Theo, it was so . . . so very beautiful. And it felt like a kind of relief, you know. A release, or something. But, what's super weird is, I was feeling it for *you*. Oh, and the sky, Theo! It was—what the hell're you watching?" The screen hummed, illuminated by colored bars.

"I don't even think this is a show," she added.

Static buzzed electric.

He answered with a sip, spilled it into his mouth. Theo's face hung heavy, droopy-eyed, mournful as a basset hound's. It was always worse this time of year. His whiskers pushed through in patches, and his coughs came out in clots. Last week, the bouncer said he found Theo in the "gentlemen's room" quaking so badly beside a urinal, he had to help him re-zip. Even Theo's sketches—the most inspired of which were slid beneath her door—had changed. Shakes rendered Teal's face grotesque. She recognized herself in caricature, nude, and sliding off the side of torn bar napkins.

"It's a miracle. A real one," she said. "It's *Mary*, Theo. And when I was sleeping, she showed me what to do."

"Put the ironing board on eBay?"

The bottle returned, drained, to the nightstand. Theo twitched around in his bathrobe and his bald spot hit the headboard. Wicked weather did this to him, Teal could tell. Her own father was lost, winters ago, to the blues. It was a protection of him that Teal projected onto Theo. Lately, she kept a close watch over her next-door neighbor, the old man who kept a close watch over her. She stayed late at the bar's deep fryer, dunking Buffalo wings and cheese sticks. Extra crispy, the way he liked them. She held the button that read, "Manager. Night bell. Use only in emergency," until a man opened in boxers and anger to take her money—$200, single bills—so Theo could sleep. She even brought swizzle sticks from the bar for Ferrah. The parrot was crazy about pink plastic, and the old man was crazy about the parrot. Through their shared wall, when morning made gray bars of the blinds, Teal listened for him wheezing on his way to the can.

"Anyways, the Virgin Mary's on my ironing board, and she showed me how to help. Are you even listening, Theo? Mary's in my goddamn linen closet!"

Ferrah stopped preening. "Goddamn!"

Wiggling ten fingers, warm at last, Teal glanced up, smooched at the cage. She was certain Ferrah would understand. The bird knew. Ferrah could feel freedom, and it was right outside the motel room. But to Theo, it all had to be explained. How could she convince him? How could she convey the lighting in her dream, the way it swirled and sifted like dust, coating everything gold? How could she show the way the sky spread, wide and hopeful? The way Mary slumped slightly in her veils, biting her lip above the ironing board, above the bird, working patiently, lovingly, ever so careful not to singe Ferrah's wings?

FERRAH

Together, they jostled her house to the floor. The girl had talons that tapped her food dish. The man twitched. His wings jerked.

"I don't know, I don't know," he said, over and over, pacing the room.

"Don't know!" shrieked Ferrah. Even though she did. She knew the creak of her own door, the swing on its tiny hinges, as well as she knew the newspaper articles that were her carpet. Midday, when he woke, the man would lift the latch to watch her strut the sink rim, then bounce onto the mini-fridge. This made a *tick-tick* beneath her toenails. This settled his shakes. Sometimes he whistled the child's song. It belonged to his baby bird who had gone. It pooled in the man's eyes, stood Ferrah's feathers on end.

But everything was different now. Her home was unhooked from the ceiling. There was apprehension all around, and she felt it where plumage poked skin. The girl's head pressed huge against the bars. It coaxed with clucks, with shiny black quills. Ferrah nodded on her porch, before hopping onto the girl's crooked perch. The tip was painted, *pretty pretty.* At the opposite end was a band of inlaid blue. She tapped it twice with her beak. It was cool on her tongue—the way turquoise should taste.

From the girl, Ferrah swooped to the television. In the columns on the screen, she recognized her own colors. For a wing-beat she considered flying smack into them. Tele-landings were always tricky—flight patterns depended upon the angle of antennae. She tried to relax, tried to unruffle, but the box whirred up through her legs, vibrating her tail. The man's door stood strange. Open with night, wide with possibility.

Out fluttered the girl, into a neon wild Ferrah could barely recall.

The parrot paused on the knob, sniffing after her at unused air. Ferrah's feet slipped, repositioned, then slipped again. The view from her swing had given a glimpse of sky, where she swung and sang to fragments. But nothing like this. Nothing like the unobstructed rush of lights and sensations that made Ferrah's tail fan from the doorknob.

The man approached. He trembled on the threshold. Ferrah flew to him, finding stable footing on his shoulder. It had been necessary, of late, to keep a close watch over him. She budged up to his neck, where tremors comforted.

Behind the girl, the man stepped out of his cage.

Wind made it difficult to keep grip. Ferrah huddled tight to the smell of man-sweat and the sharp nectar he sipped. Rain blew in slants. She sang, "What the fuck, what the fuck," again and again into his ear. A few of his feathers whiskered out, tickling her cheek.

"Pretty! Love my pretty! Goddamn bird!" When she opened her beak, in poured night. The breeze swallowed cold and new. It ruffled her tail, lifted his collar. It was too much to resist.

Ferrah loosened her claws. She hovered momentarily when one snagged on wool, then rose. Beating at rain gusts, flapping at black, she looked from the man to the girl, then back to the man. Startled by the exhilaration of simply letting go.

She gyred above them, circling, cawing invitation. But they didn't fly or follow. As if they had never learned how. The man squinted at her, bringing a wing above his beak in salute. Ferrah cried out once over the Blue Moon Motel, once over the stunned figures who were, finally, stilled.

Ascending, the parrot arced a rainbow against the clouds. Her blue feathered with falling water. Far below, she saw the girl lean into the man. He held onto her, as they grew smaller and smaller.

FAYE

Spring arrived early with a string of break-ins. With an outbreak of fear. Someone was moving across Cody County, opening windows to dream in other people's beds. The invasions were polite enough. The toothpaste was always recapped, the sheets always retucked. Valuables were never stolen (nothing beyond a microwave meal or a pay-per-view movie), yet the town mourned its we-never-lock-our-doors mentality. Trust plummeted. Gun sales spiked. A few friends of friends (whom Faye knew about personally) had interrupted the intruder—spooning out their canned soup or bubbling up their bathtub. But the trespasser invariably slipped away.

Through the center of town, there snaked a long, cold lake. It wave-licked the historic district, two trailer parks, and field after field of pale grass. Faye heard the intrusions began on the south shore, where the snow-burrowed bungalows of "vacation home row" sat vacant and waiting all winter long. Where hide-a-keys hid by front doors in fake rocks. The local paper even gave him a nickname (which, for a crook, means you've made it big): "The House-Sit Bandit."

But Faye had no space, in heart or home, for uninvited guests. In fact, no one had visited for years. Outside her apartment, alley cats scavenged, hedges shadowed, and— somewhere in the murk by the lake—The House-Sit Bandit crept. Her dresser held panties stitched in the '50's, little sachets of potpourri, and a cylinder of just-in-case mace. Above her door, an alarm system blinked. Above her bed, a bare bulb burned away night.

Days spent at Daryl's Department Store passed best. Which, for Faye, meant a fast lapse from one task to the next—folding then refolding a cardigan, smiling then un-smiling as a customer turned to leave. She'd refused the meager retirement offered her, preferring the employment benefits of distraction. It was window display work that had, for three decades, brought comfort and calm. Stretches of uninterrupted nonfeeling. Nine-to-fives insulated from mind and mood. The mannequins had been the same man-nequins for years, and when Faye moved them, they never asked her to be moved in turn. Actually, they never asked her anything at all.

The figures were cool against Faye's fingers. Bald-headed and Barbie-crotched, their plastic was hard, blank. Expres-sionless as nylon-sheathed thieves. They were rigid and lightweight and looked great in any outfit. There were even kid mannequins. Faye liked to arrange the adults around them, in matching attire, in various postures of protection.

Driving from Daryl's, she squinted red at the road. Her eyes were blinked dry from double shifts and three days awake. From predawns awaiting the scratch of the screen, the whine of the window latch.

Her Buick turned off the highway, on impulse, on the outskirts of town. She followed a sign, through dust and dusk, to a store that was a house. To a house that was a store. Gravel ground beneath her tires, while beige grit settled on her windshield. She braked beside a limo. It looked road-worn, haunted as a hearse. In layers of grime, odd hieroglyphs had been fingered: squiggles, like waves or wings; two triangles exchanging smiles; an S-shape.

The house had peeling paint and shingles missing like teeth. It was the kind of house realtors never bother to list. The kind of house, which, decades ago, may have held laughter, a pantryful of flour and sugar, a family circling an oak table—but not anymore. Faye could tell that all it hosted now were drafts, termites, ghosts.

and some loony with a taxi

Faye patted her curls, silver swirls in the rearview mirror. Stepping into evening, double-checking the car (locked, both times), she nearly tripped over the pink nub of a pogo stick. Price-tagged objects sprawled across the yard. Strung from the gutter, a homemade windchime twirled, clinking tin above boxes of books. A Raggedy Ann doll rode an exercise bike beside a toilet. Sprouting out of a flowerpot, a prosthetic leg.

From beneath the porch, a small form skipped, gripping a tulip. The girl looked malnourished, orphanesque. Shirtless against the sliding sun, she paused, stared straight through Faye, then darted into a thicket of engine parts and tires stacked to towers.

feral

Faye trapped the word for a moment. But it, too, slipped away.

What had pulled her from the road? What pulled a bill, minutes later, from her purse folds? Faye couldn't say. Maybe it was loneliness, mixed with allergy meds and fear. Or the darkness of her apartment. Or the ribcage, pale and delicate, disappearing into a maze of metal.

The lamp was meant for Faye. She knew it before she reached it, overturned in overgrown grass. With a gold body and no bulb, the unlit light called her forward, through a graveyard of belongings. She fingered the shade, which was edge-frayed to tassels, and imagined safety. A warmth that would radiate security. A well-being that could be seen from the street.

just a nightlight for dead hours

"Slashed this morning. Down to ten bucks." Faye spun to see a face, staring from the porch. It wore three-week stubble and potholes for pockmarks. It belonged to a man as big as a bear. Nodding nervously, she climbed two steps to where he stood.

A paw lifted the lamp for her.

Faye touched her curls, then her clutch purse. "This is probably just what I need, you know?"

The man grunted, turning to rummage through a garbage bag.

"It's the perfect height, really . . . should fit right behind my bed stand."

"Sadie, dammit!" he shouted, though there was no one in sight.

Faye jumped, looked toward the yard, the limo, the

scrap labyrinth beyond.

"She's *obsessed* with bubble-wrap." The man held up a sheet of transparent skin. Every blister had been popped. "Sorry. I'll find something else to pad your light. Cash only, by the way."

Straight home, through a haze of meds, four deadbolts, and a hall that smelled of mold, Faye carried her buy. The huge man had wrapped it with half of a mattress pad, ripped ragged down the center. When she peeled back duct tape, the foam unfolded like someone stretching. It flushed the color of flesh. Sitting at the center, the lamp flashed brass. She set it aside. At that moment, only the mattress mattered. In its squish, Faye could feel the fibers of sleep. She placed the pad on top of the comforter, then curled around herself, comforted at long last.

Form-fitting, the foam seemed to breathe beneath Faye. She'd seen the commercials: "Astronaut tested and pressure absorbing. Half of life is spent dreaming, so you deserve the softest sleep . . . You deserve a Posture-Slumber!"

What the ads never mentioned, however, was the mattress' tenderness. Propped against the headboard, haloed by hair-curlers, Faye understood sensitivity. Sensitivity as strength—the way the word was intended. The mattress was impressionable. It held a muscle memory, an imprint of its last dreamer. A gingerbread cutout with heels, and elbows, and ass, all missing—but still there somehow. Sleeping ghostly beside Faye. She dared her fingertips to trace the outline, the negative. The void of whoever had been, or continued to be.

On her back beside the indent, Faye felt safe. Safe, and

sure it wasn't the new light. Her day came drifting back then, in strange shapes and shifting impressions: a man's throat growl, dust sifting, a tulip dropped red on gravel. Someone needed to be notified about that child, poor thing. It was only right.

Faye pressed her shoulders into foam. Slipping sleepward, she started to think,

it's our padding that protects us

But then Faye thought nothing at all—already too far off.

BEVERLY

Bev worked weeknights at O'Blivion's. As beer-slinger and babysitter, fry cook and behind-the-bar shrink. Some days she felt spent, washed out. Peroxide-dyed and wrinkled beyond recognition. Her smile, mirrored in beer taps, made the charcoal around her eyes crinkle. Laugh lines made her mouth parenthetical.

O'Blivion's was the oldest tavern in town, the darkest, set deep and narrow into brick. There, Bev crumpled time, noon 'til midnight, like a worn dollar bill. Hours into weeks, shifts into years. The bar was a dive, the headfirst kind. The only place you could get a black eye, a leg up in local politics, and a piece of ass—all in the same night. Where wisecracks passed as currency, STDs as fast as PCP. Where people felt better for being together.

"Karaoke Monday" meant cases of Bud Light and the spins. It meant impromptu line dancing and incorrect lyrics. It meant mullets. The tavern hosted epic fistfights and public love on the pinball machine. Weddings, blind dates, wakes. Fat, drunk men, sobbing for their mommies. But

Bev, a twenty-year bar vet, knew how to handle such entanglements—all while carrying five pints and a tune.

Lil' Smokies swelled in the deep fryer, splitting pink skins. They splattered scars onto Bev's forearms. Silver dots she would connect with a pen during customer lulls, into constellations. The jukebox glowed, and her hairspray glinted neon green. She only used Super 16-Hour Hold. An extra aerosol can was stashed behind the bar, shelved below the beef jerky and the urinal cakes. It kept Bev's bangs upright and shot feet farther than mace. Reaching for Ranch dressing, she kick-closed the fridge door. The spike of her heel left another dent.

On swivel stools, slumped over the counter, six men watched and sipped.

awww, look how they're curled . . . like lil' old fetuses

She wiped a beer ring from the bar. They all sipped again.

should rename this place, "Womb"—we could pump liquor through tubes, heartbeats through speakers

The thought brought Bev a strange comfort, then a smile. Merv, who'd been sitting and swigging since noon, assumed it was for him.

"New skirt?" His nose was veined red, ready to fall off.

"Nope," said Bev, tugging denim to cover her thighs. The Guinness she was pouring overfoamed. But Merv was too sad to be a pervert, too lost to lust. He had a bulldog named Meatball who waited and wailed outside the bar. He had a son who died young. He had a few too many on Bev's shifts, rolling teardrops with tobacco. She made sure to wink false lashes his way, to guess at his crosswords.

"Four down is 'wallow.'" She tapped a press-on against his paper.

Merv shook a smoke under his mustache. The hair was stained yellow where he sucked. "But it has to start with an 's,' Sweetheart."

"Want chicken tenders, Merv?"

In response, the edges of his mustache lifted. Bev could only assume that, deep beneath, Merv had a mouth. She was glad to feed it, glad to care for all souls in O'Blivion's. They brought thirst and every appetite imaginable. Not to mention story after story of suffering, like a teetering stack of books.

At the karaoke machine, a biker coughed a cowboy song into the microphone. Backfeed screeched. Next to the "stage," a square space delineated by floor tape, two couples twirled around and around. On top of the pool table, a woman danced in a bra and a daze. All alone and cloud-capped by Marlboro smoke.

Beverly dropped the wire basket into the fryer. She stared down at grease churning. She inhaled its heavy, bready odor. Hissing in oil, dancing at a boil, the meat looked shriveled, gray.

christ almighty, they're chicken scrotums

"Ranch or ketchup, Merv?" she shouted over her shoulder.

He answered over the music, "Are you ever super aware of your ticker? Of your heart, is what I'm sayin'. Like just noticing it might make it quit?" A pink tongue licked from his beard to run the length of a rolling paper. "Ketchup. Please."

Al, who drank in dentures and plaid two stools down,

told him to shut the fuck up with his ticker talk.

"Mind your own guts," said Merv.

"Trying," said Al, grinning wrinkles and white gums.

From his upper lip, Merv flicked a flake of tobacco.

Bev watched in the mirror behind the bar. Years of slinging beer had revealed the fragility of grown men, their schoolyard susceptibility to fighting words. If Al and Merv kept this up—what had been escalating for weeks—both would make the 86 list. The names of those banned from O'Blivion's were noted on post-its and stuck beside the cash register. It was an ever-changing Rolodex of regulars, most of whom (with the passing of time and tips) earned their re-welcome. Offenses were often forgotten. Post-its eventually lost their stick to drift behind the deep fryer, where roaches scuttled and no one ever swept.

Merv's dinner spat and crackled from its vat, as Bev puckered her lips at the mirror. She popped a bottle top, cocked her head. Every hair stayed put. Low light—and just the right angle—let her forget frown lines, skin that freckled and sagged. In the reflection, a lighter clicked sparks. Merv shook it by his ear, where more white hair whiskered out.

"Wouldn't ya know it." He lifted the lighter in one hand, the beer in the other—both inhaled to empty.

shave his face, and it would disappear

Beverly walked toward him with a full Budweiser and a book of matches.

"Cheers," she said.

"Alls I was trying to say is that sometimes my chest, it kinda like compresses and stuff. Then it pumps real hard. Against this flapping." He touched his shirt where he imagined his heart. "Like it's collapsing, ya know, onto something sorta frantic."

Bev stood still a moment, blinking. "Damn if I'm a doc, but do you think you're experiencing some kinda—some kinda cardio . . . whatcha-ma-callums?"

Merv pushed the bottle into his beard. "Yup. Yup, I think that's it exactly. My insides. They got a mind of their own."

Bev rarely considered the inner-workings of anything, never mind her own good body. It had served her (not to mention others) for four decades and was barely worse for wear. She could still split a bar fight better than any bouncer. She could still love hard through the long night, then stretch strong into tomorrow's shift.

She leaned in. For privacy, for a peek of cleavage. "How many years, huh? Since he, since your son . . . left? Maybe you just need—"

"How long?" Merv laughed. His cigarette ashed onto the bar. "I'd love to meet the dimwit who started that rumor, the one where time heals wounds, or whatever." He glared down the bar, as if Al were to blame for the cliché.

poor guy, guard-dog loyal to his own sadness

Bev bit at a fake nail. She could smell chicken tenders. "What I mean is—"

"Nah. Time's just another space we can't cross, just another long-ass distance. Stretching out and away, ya know, away from all that's got lost." To show this expanse, Merv extended an arm into spiraling smoke.

"Maybe skip outta town for a bit?" The fryer made growling sounds behind her, like an unfed gut. The oil gurgled, roiled. It wafted a scorched odor, threatening to boil over. "Maybe this place, this lake, holds too much. Too many memories . . ."

"I got those, yeah. Memories aplenty."

She nodded encouragement, "Good, good," snapping cinnamon gum to close the subject.

"Thing is though, all the wrong ones're stuck in here." Merv tapped his temple. "Awful. Nightmare stuff. What I want back, I can't quite get . . . the shape his smile made first time behind the wheel. Or the weight of him when he was real little and warm and squirmy in my arms. . . ." Merv's flannel sleeves came together to make a cradle. He rocked air. "Hell. Can't pull *those* memories back up. They get deeper forgotten, deeper every time I fuckin' try."

Bev scanned the room. Table three was brooding over no brew, and a ball was stuck in the bowels of the pool table. Again.

"Be right back with your tenders, 'kay?"

From the end of the bar, she took two orders. Back to Merv and his misplaced memories, she took her time. Their exchange had put Bev on edge. Such topics remained decidedly beyond discussion. This, she could control—as well as she held control over O'Blivion's 'til closing. Death was, for Bev, life's greatest embarrassment. To be splayed out like that, slack-jawed, for all to gawk at. To be so exposed.

how very vulnerable it makes you

Bev shook her head to shake the thought. She tossed it with a bottle cap, but not before an image of Merv's boy filled her mind. The way the paper said he was found. The way he had let himself be lost—in winter, in his father's basement, in his own blown brains and shit. Bev heard the fryer sputter. She hurried to check on Merv's forgotten meal.

Trifocals sat on his newspaper, flashing empty lenses. Cross-eyed over four across, he squinted toward an answer.

"Beverly, Honey? Bev, Hon, need yer help here: five-letter L-word for a mythic, Greek river. Any guesses?"

The bar phone rang.

Bev put plastic to her ear, answering as she always did: "Thank you for calling O'Blivion's, he's not here. . . ."

On the line was the first tourist of the season. The year's first out-of-towner to mistake O'Blivion's for a desirable dining option.

"Um, no. No, we don't take reservations." Bev raised her eyebrows, then her voice, for the benefit of those at the bar. "Yeah, it's pretty much seat yourself." She cupped a hand over the mouthpiece to mute her laugh, to silence customer taunts.

Earl, who cut lumber up-lake, yelled, "We'll show 'em to their seats!"

"Got no reservations 'bout that," said Al.

Bev hushed them, finger to lips. "Menu? Uh, no, but I can pretty much deep fry whatever. . . ." She examined her hair in the mirror.

holding strong

"Yup. Yup, well, we're on Main, dead-center of Cody." Looking up, Beverly made note of whose reflection needed a refill. Over his PBR, under his breath, Al was mumbling something at Merv. Both men sat stiff. She watched Al raise a hand, in slow gesture, to his own smirk. The thumb and pointer-finger were L-ed into the shape of a gun.

Suddenly, Merv was standing, swaying. His bar stool

tottered on two legs before it tipped to the floor with a wood thud. The row of drinkers turned to see him, hunch-shouldered and trudging toward the men's room.

Into the phone, she said, "Listen, gotta run, we're slammed. Yeah, that's right. . . yeah. Just past Daryl's Department Store, if you wanna stop in for—"

What Bev heard, and what Bev saw, shared no synchronicity. The crack of Merv's head against the corner pocket, where an eight ball wobbled, was one event. The slow motion of his fall, against a crowd in fast forward, was another altogether. Then came a shout—"Merv, man, you okay?"— and the shame of inaction, the stasis of panic. Bev turned a full circle before wrapping her mind around the situation. She dropped the receiver.

Regulars were steadying Merv to his feet, bandaging his face with their bandanas. Bev wet a towel under the faucet. Pushing past a hand that waved a pull-tab, she circled the bar to the pool table. Merv swayed at a half-stand.

"Here, take my arm. Shit. Lemme call you a cab, or something." Alcohol rendered Merv ragdoll-limp, which was surely why he hadn't shattered. She reached the cloth toward his forehead, but he batted it away.

"I walk. Me and meatball, we always walk." The bush of his left eyebrow was catching blood, beginning to show a crust brown.

"Let's rest up then. In a booth, huh? Just for a sec."

Beverly settled him onto the nearest seat. There he slumped, staring straight ahead, while she dialed the number taped to the back of the taps. It was scrawled with a sharpie pen, labeled TAXI. She returned to the booth.

"Wanna glass of water? Cab's just right up the road, should swoop by for you super soon. Before you know it. Water?"

"My check . . . and my crossword." The old man searched the dim, as if the room had been rearranged, as if his puzzle had switched seats.

"Pay me tomorrow, all right?" With a good grip on Merv's suspenders, she guided him back to the barstool, where his newspaper waited with a pile of bottle caps, then to the door, where Meatball waited with drool dripping from her underbite.

"Okay, then. . ." she said. When Bev released Merv, suspender straps snapped against the bones of his back.

Through the window and its peeling beer ads, through the evening and its fading light, she could see the limo. It was revving loud out of a dirt-caked hood. From the passenger side, a little face stared back.

that odd kid again

The girl pressed her mouth against the limo window, inflating both cheeks like a puffer fish. She slid down then, deep into the bucket seat and out of sight. A circle of breath shrank on the glass.

"See? You're ride's here," said Beverly, but Merv had already turned.

She watched him step, gray and dazed, into new spring. He squinted at bright like someone just born. Like an old soul delivered.

LUX

Lux only entered O'Blivion's on occasion, and only when necessary. When the customer who needed cabbing was too wasted to walk. When the bartender, whose name he could never remember, smacked gum into the receiver, called him "Hon," and said he'd better come inside for this one. Lux would sooth the boozer with how-are-yas, then steady him, arm over shoulder like a wounded soldier, refusing whatever frou-frou beverage the barmaid offered. Lux preferred his drinks battery-acid strong and alone. Sipped between pipe puffs on the front porch.

But tonight, Lux needed people, however unbearable. He needed the jukebox deafening, pints overflowing, customer service underwhelming. Teensy-weensy cocktail straws, and small talk with that big-titted beerslinger. Whatever her name was.

The limousine coughed to a stop beside a fire hydrant. Lux killed the engine. A parking spot was wherever the vehicle fit, rarely where the law saw fit. It was well past twelve, and Sadie lay sprawled across the back seat, out cold. Knees splayed, cheek pressed against the safety buckle. When she woke, a square would be imprinted on her freckles. She looked wilted. Her blonde was ashen, her mouth open. She was passed out like a drunk, snoring like a lumberjack.

A stoplight hung overhead, swinging on a wire in the wind. It flashed in four directions. It pulsed at two-second intervals, strobing red over the child. Bringing her in and out of focus, again and again. Sadie's eyes were rolled back like a doll's, her lids half-lifted in a way Lux found slightly creepy. She always slept like this. Seemingly hypnotized, and just as difficult to rouse. The girl mumbled, "*Now?*" and her face twitched, twice, as if with a tick. The corners of her mouth turned up, her eye-whites glinted in the dim. She sighed, pale lashes fluttering like moths. Lux ached to see what she saw. Sadie would dream straight through his whiskey. Through one beer, maybe two.

Lux brushed the child's face with the back of his hand.

sleep sweet, Papa's just a few feet away

He locked the doors (all eight) and crossed the street, glancing over his shoulder at the limo. It blinked back at him, black-red-black. It held his whole world.

Smoke and music wafted from the bar. A lilting laugh and an odor like deep fried jockstrap. Stapled to the entrance was a Miller High Life poster. It pictured a woman sitting coy on a crescent moon. It read "The Champagne of Beers," and curled at the edges like an ancient scroll. Lux ran a hand through his thinning hair, then through his thickening scruff, thinking of warm whiskey and sleepy Sadie.

O'Blivion's was dark and dank as a sea cave. Shells, sucked of peanuts, crunched under Lux's boots. Shadows clung to the bar, belly up, and shapes fixed to booths like barnacles. Around the dance floor, figures drifted, faces obscured. They moved to a bluegrass tune—or to their own internal rhythms—irregular as waves. At this hour, only hardcore drinkers remained: weeknight regulars, sleepwalkers, barstool warriors. In the far corner, a silhouette was slamming a palm against the pinball machine, swearing. His shouts could be heard between harmonica notes.

"—god-fucking-ball-damned-quarter-shit—"

At the end of the bar, a woman sat with tinfoil rectangles creased in her hair. Arranged like small solar panels, they flashed in beat with the jukebox. Lux wondered what sort of energy they stored.

As he approached, the woman said, "'Kay, one more. But then I'm goin' home. S'posed to warsh this stuff out after half hour. How long I been here?"

The bartender—hairsprayed, squeezed into faded jeans—shrugged and set down a shot. The liquid was translucent, brimming.

"Thanks, Bev. After this, though, I'm leavin'. To warsh this shit out."

Bev . . . that's right, that's her name, Bev

Lux pulled out a barstool and pressed his bulk into the row of drinkers. Beside him, a man made of beard was reading a newspaper, grunting. It was open to the obits. His facial hair was frizzed, as in a cartoon electrocution. The bristle sprouted, cheekbone to jawbone. Above his left eyebrow, a gash was healing, peeling pink. Without turning the man said, "My obstetrician died."

"Beg pardon?"

"My gynie, my gyno . . . whatever. You want one more, huh?" he asked, oblivious to the fact that Lux hadn't yet been served. The beard nodded, encouraging another pour. It hid his lips, whiskered into a mustache which curlicued at the tips. "My doc, the one who delivered me, I mean. The first person to see me, to touch me. Ever. Dead." The man took a crinkled pack of American Spirits from his pocket. "Spooky stuff."

Lux said nothing, spooked himself. With a raised palm, he tried to flag down Bev, but she turned to take an order. Below her crop top, above the pinch of her pants, a fat roll pudged. It looked soft, tender, pale yellow as butter.

The newspaper, now turned to a crossword, slid in front of Lux. He looked down at the puzzle, then up at the man. Somewhere under the hair, he may have been grinning. Or simply staring, straight-faced, Lux couldn't tell. There was too much beard to be sure. The man tapped the page.

"Any good at these thingies?"

Lux shrugged.

"They're my sanity."

in that case, do a few more

"Beverly likes 'em, too, don'tcha, Darlin'?" Teetering a tower of stacked pints, Bev stopped walking, thrust out a hip. She looked at Lux.

"Oh, hey. Didn't see you. Rex, right?"

"Um, no. No, it's Lux."

"Sorry, Sugar. Don't take it personal."

"I take everything personally. Can I get a Maker's? Double. Neat."

"Sure thing, Hon. Merv here bothering you?" Winking,

she reached over the man's beer to tickle his beard.

The whiskey appeared, moments later, a single shot. Not neat. Its ice was already melting. In the mirror behind the bar, Lux could see the man, baffled above his puzzle, stroking his face fuzz. He could see the glint of the Guinness tap, the concentric rings of the dartboard, his own stare glaring back. Lux liked to watch himself. To study the ripple of his jowls, the wrinkles around his eyes, the rubber face he'd always been told was grotesque. It was endlessly fascinating, being both watcher and watched. It was a habit at which he often got caught, then got embarrassed.

Lux tossed back his glass, head thrown fast, in a motion one might associate with hysterical laughter—were it not for the sunken expression. Whiskey drained, then burned. An avalanche of ice cubes buried his mouth. Lux opened for one, letting the freeze numb his tongue and gums. He bit down. With each crunch, an electric twinge shot through a rear molar. There came a twang of pain, which Lux categorized as high-pitched, glacial blue. The sensation brought a perverse pleasure. He bit again, wondered when the decayed bastard would fall out. Lux hated dentists—their steel trays and drill bits, their bibs for spit and blood—wouldn't even make an appointment for Sadie's baby teeth.

Lux thought of the girl, all alone in the limo. He shifted on the stool, crunched more ice. Dentists were sadists—he had no dough for one, anyway.

can't afford my own rotting

Setting down the glass, Lux thought of the kid's incisors—sharp, jagged, slightly misaligned. Kitten teeth. She was always thrilled when one jiggled lose. A total of four had been pulled from under her pillow, hairy-fairied away. Replaced with a buffalo nickel, a seashell, a mood ring, a velvet ribbon the color and feel of melted chocolate. Chomping another cube, he remembered Sadie's terror the first time she felt a tooth wiggle: "Papa Bear, I'm *dying*!" The memory made Lux cough, then stand suddenly, stiffly, nearly knocking his barstool to the floor.

Something was wrong. Something had happened. To Sadie. He knew it. He could feel it—a wrenching at his core, a twisting in his belly, which radiated panic in pulses through his nervous system. Lux charged toward the door, ignoring Bev's shout.

"Hey, Lex, you gonna pay for that, or what!"

The night was lightweight, soft-breezing spring. Somewhere, a dog was howling, long and lonesome as a wolf. Lux moved toward the limo, reeling with the inkling it was empty. With each step, he grew more and more sure of this. Sadie and Lux had always sensed each other's presence, dreaded each other's absence. The kid hated hide-and-go-seek. While she never failed to find him, she always felt terrific anxiety in the trying. His pace quickened.

By the time Lux reached the taxi, he was running, stumbling to see the vacant backseat, the space where Sadie once slept. Where she'd awoken, terrified and alone. It would be impossible to determine which direction she'd wandered. Overhead, the four-way blinked and blinked.

A car passed, headlighting the window where Lux cupped his hands, pressed his face. The glass was grimy, gritted. Inside the cab, dark turned red. The pleather seat gleamed—empty, save for a bikinied Barbie sitting upright and safety-buckled.

Lux lost all sense of space and reason then, dropping to both knees, checking beneath the limousine, even looking starward. As if the kid opted to rocket elsewhere.

"Sadie!" Her name echoed down Main Street, seemed to hop the thin lake, lose its way through silhouettes of trees and hills.

"Sadie! Sadie, Baby!" Spinning, Lux began to unlock the driver's-side door. Then stopped. Curled in the kicked-back seat, Sadie snoozed beneath the steering wheel, socks pressed to the gearshift.

His eyes filled, stung, then spilled. In that moment, in that after-midnight, Sadie became mortal. This realization was, to Lux, nearly fatal. He stood, unmoving, watching the girl: her slack lips, her catsup-stained sweater, her legs frail as a sparrow's. For a full five minutes, Lux stayed, transfixed by the rise and fall of Sadie's ribcage, the bone knobs of her knees, the dark of her mouth. He pushed a palm to the window, held it there, then hurried back toward O'Blivion's to pay his tab.

At the door, a bulldog sat leashed to a bike rack, whimpering. The woman in the tinfoil helmet brushed past, mumbling something about booze and her roots.

Bev was pouring a pint with one hand, wagging a press-on nail with the other. "You're fuckin' lucky I didn't chase you, Rex. Only reason's 'cause I know you'll be back soon, for a customer. Where'd you buy that taxi, anyway?"

"Can I get my check?"

Beverly blew a marble-size bubble with her gum, pointed to where he'd been sitting.

On the bar was his tab. On his stool was a girl, swiveling

side to side like a youngster at an old-time soda fountain.

Lux stared.

Her movements were jerky, impulsive. They had an involuntary quality—as if her body reacted to every impulse, every fast-passing thought. A gold beer foamed white froth on the bar in front of her. She tipped it to her lips, and the coaster stayed stuck to the bottom of the pint. She had no grace yet, no womanly delicacy—only the spaces these powers would one day fill. Black hair spilled down her spine. Even in barroom dim, he noticed highlights running through, mahogany and gilt streaks which reminded Lux of wood grain. She was trying to light a smoke, sucking one end like a candy cigarette. She was puppy-clumsy, awkward. She was stunning.

numinous

Lux didn't know what the word meant, but he was sure it described her. She seemed fresh to him—clean, newborn. Lux imagined he could smell laundry drying, white and crisp, on a long line in the wind. Yet, drawing closer, the only odor was the deep fryer, mixed with some sort of cologne spray for tweens.

"'Scuze me," he said, squeezing between the bearded man's plaid and the girl's bare arm. She wore a red dress the length of a nightshirt. It evoked more than it covered. She looked directly at Lux. Her eyes were penciled with sable, which smudged into silver, which blurred into baby blue. Her lipstick was slick, lacquered, applied thick. It left a pink kiss on the rim of the glass. She looked like an angel-faced boy-child, new to drag. Or a little girl who raided her mother's makeup drawer.

christ jesus, don't they card in here?

"Thought you'd left me to foot your bill." Her voice was deeper than he'd expected. Razor-edged and not entirely attractive. The beer foam had left a line above her mouth, much like a milk mustache. From a plastic package of crackers, the girl was breaking off pieces of Saltines, spraying little spitlets onto his outstretched wrist. Crumbs fell to her thighs where Lux wouldn't let his eyes go. He could have dropped to his knees right there, begging at her feet, scratching for scraps.

"Nah, I was coming back, I just. . . ." Lux dug in his pocket for a balled-up bill. He slapped a ten on the bar, tried not to look at her.

She said, "How are you?" and seemed to mean it. A pimple on her chin crusted with cover-up.

"Too close to call."

"Know whatcha mean." She sipped again, slurping. The girl held Lux without touching, cooling him, fanning him out like a hand of cards. "I totally know. Though I'd have never thought to say it that way."

"You wouldn't?"

"Nope."

"Well . . . me neither then." He grinned, almost as wide as he would at Sadie.

Sadie

Lux seized up. He nodded briefly at the beard, then at the girl (the girl who couldn't have been a decade older than his own kid), and turned toward the door. Walking away, he wondered at one's ability to sink and soar so rapidly, to fly and fall so quickly. In such a short span of time, in such a close proximity of space. Lux once read that the highest point in the U.S. is just 80 miles from the lowest. His boot heel crunched a peanut shell.

Behind him, he heard Beverly say, "'Nother beer, Teal?"

Teal, Teal, Teal

Lux stepped into night—into a dark which seemed, somehow, bright. Somehow shiny, brand new.

THEO

Blue Moon Motel, 2:00 a.m. Monday, maybe Tuesday. Theo was in bed, drinking wine, drawing Teal's outline, when he heard them through the wall. When he heard Teal laugh—one long, winnowy peal—more like a mare than a girl. When he heard the man. Not his words, exactly, but the rise and fall of his syllables, the cadence of his sentences, the scrape of his consonants against plaster. Then silence.

the maintenance guy—surly old bastard works all sorts of hours

Theo sensed something unsound in this logic, but was too drunk to sort it out. Too focused on cocktail napkin sketches. Lately, he'd been pacing obsessively, drinking excessively, pounding everything alcoholic but mouthwash and Windex.

From next door, there came a thonk-bonk-thonk, cryptic and rhythmic.

her mini fridge must be broken again, second time this week

Not that Teal would care. The kid had little need for a fridge, as all she seemed to eat were Ritalin and Skittles.

With a quick swig of shiraz, his ballpoint poised, Theo continued to draw: girl parts under stage lights, stilettos under disco-ball eyes. Teal from behind. Teal from the side. Teal, when she thought no one was watching, adjusting a slipping strap over one shoulder.

In the adjacent room, a drawer or cupboard door slammed. Theo picked up the bottle, held it angled to his mouth 'til it emptied.

Something dropped. Another thud.

The maintenance man let out a muffled grunt, like someone muttering into a pillow. There was a metallic clatter—his wrench or screwdriver, no doubt.

should replace her refrigerator altogether

As a rule, Teal never saw customers outside the club. She had never once, since moving into the motel, brought anyone home. Theo would have known. Theo would have heard. This was neither a safety concern, nor an allegiance to some strippers' code of conduct. It was neither caution nor professionalism. Teal was too impulsive for prudence, too reckless for any effort toward etiquette. Her idea of security (when high-heeling through alleyways) was to hold a key, serrated and ready, between two knuckles. Her idea of vocational protocol (when slinking through dim) was to introduce herself before a lap dance.

No, the absence of guests was neither for protection, nor propriety. It was either for Theo's sake—he liked to think—or for the fact that Teal hated men. All men, except Theo. Theo, and the dead father she refused to speak of, save to say: "He was very tall, and very sad, and would always peel the skin off the grapes I ate, 'cause I like 'em better that way. Really, Theo, every single grape. Can you imagine? He loved me that much."

Yes, Theo could imagine.

Her dad's name—Reb—was inked at the base of Teal's back. A cursive script, tattooed to the curve of her spine. An amateur's handiwork, slightly off-center, which rippled and shrank as she arched on stage. Theo had no idea what happened to her father, other than that something took him slowly, brutally. And that she sat by his side the entire time.

The tattoo was never included in Theo's portraits of Teal. The drawings belonged to him, and he refused to acknowledge the tat's existence. Ribs 'n' Racks almost hadn't hired her because of it. The manager said that the marking was exclusionary, that patrons would assume she'd been branded by a lover. Dancers were to appear available, somehow virginal in their seduction, somehow attainable in their anonymity. (Which was laughable, as many worked the pole at various stages of pregnancy, or were sagging grocery baggers, whom everyone knew, from the local Sack n' Snack.) Customers at the club, however, didn't seem to mind Teal's tattoo. But Theo did.

Above him hung an empty birdcage. It held seed shells and a guano-splattered editorial section. Beside him sat an empty wine bottle. It held air and an acidic smell. Theo forgot the state of both. He whistled upward, lifted drained shiraz to his mouth. An astringent drip hit his lip, chased by a crumb of cork. Theo swallowed both. Silence came from the cage.

gone, jesus, all gone

He started to sketch again, quick lines which made

scritch-scratch sounds against the cocktail napkin: Teal bent back, posing burlesque, her body in arabesque, arched and aimed as a bow. Teal in profile, close-up and clear. Teal from a distance, in motion, a squiggle mark with long hair and limbs caught mid-dip. Theo had just begun to lose himself again, when there was a bump against the wall. He jumped, set down the pen.

Next door, Teal was talking loud and fast, stilettoing over bathroom linoleum, while the male voice was laughing. A laugh that made Theo's skin tighten, his mouth turn down.

definitely not the maintenance man

Agitated, Theo scraped the nails of one hand, back and forth, over his scalp, then checked for blood. With the other hand, he held the bar napkin close to his face.

no, no that's not right at all

The proportions were wrong, the pen strokes palsied. Through layers of paper, one drawing bled onto the next, giving motion to form, instability to shape. Fixed as she was, in ink and Theo's stare, Teal appeared to waver. Like a figure walking a stretch of blazing pavement—miraging, finally, into nothing. Blue stained his fingertips, the hem of the bedspread. Theo rubbed a cobalt smudge onto the pillow.

He thought it a strange experience to draw someone a wall away—an act that embodies the dualism of all aesthetic endeavors. The subject exists: present, pliable, ink-line reliable, elastic to every creative whim. And yet she remains absent, unknowable, somehow impossible. The auditory component to Teal's nearness, the grate of her sentences, sent a spasm of anger through Theo. He massaged his neck, kneading tendons that roped and knotted. Teal's voice taunted him. Her words were blurred, muddled and jumbled as underwater muttering. Yet Theo was certain he recognized syntax—the pound of a noun, the vault of a verb. Intonation and rhythm seemed to make meaning.

A string of syllables, all stressed, came from the man.

Teal's reply was one word.

His response was trochaic, a braying.

Theo stood. He windmilled once to remain upright, then walked to the sink, picked up a motel cup, and wobbled back toward the bed. The glass was cold in his hand, crusted around the rim with toothpaste lip-marks. He pressed it to the wall.

this always works in movies

Ear to cup, cup to wall, Theo heard nothing. Nothing but a rise-and-fall whirr, like waves couched in a conch, which he took to be the sluicing of his own brain fluid. His own thoughts sloshing.

come on, where are ya?

Maybe they'd left quickly, closed the door quietly. Perhaps something else was happening entirely. Small as Theo was (hockey height, jockey weight), he felt like a wrecking ball. Like he could plow through floral wallpaper, through layers of insulation, through brick or cinderblock. And why the hell not? Theo's thud would at least communicate his state, his disapproval of the present situation. Idiot-drunk, he backed up for a running start.

A framed print saved him. A watercolor, of course. It was an awful piece of wall art: a lake (much like the one in town) which snaked through a spring day, through hills that rolled gentle and ocher. He saw, then, that two figures stood on the far shore. They were soft-brushed, stick-style, one bent slightly in what looked to Theo like sorrow. The color scheme was off, the technique fit for a community crafts fair. He glanced at the painting often enough—on the way to the shitter—but had never noticed the human shapes, the slope of those small shoulders, hunched as the hills.

Theo forgot to smash through the wall. He also forgot the wine was gone. Turning, he lifted the bottle for another sip.

blasted

Neon filtered through slits in the blinds, from the vacancy sign, whose letters circled into a baby blue moon. It made bars across his bed, light stripes that caged the length of the mattress, part of the carpet. Stumbling toward the window, he parted plastic slats with his finger. In the parking lot, nothing moved. No sound through the screen, no wind in the lone tree. A pickup truck was paralleled between a dumpster and a fence, a limousine glowed indigo under the motel sign. Overhead, a streetlamp burned out. The limo changed shades, darkening to deep sea blue.

In a stupor and boxer shorts, Theo stood staring. At the taxi, at the crack in the windshield, the stretch between the front and rear fenders, the tread-bare tires. It looked like a caricature of a car (a '70s station wagon or hearse) sketched in elongated exaggeration.

Across the hood was the word TAXI—written either by a preschooler, or by someone suffering from withdrawals. The passenger-side door had been painted red. Emergency red. Warning red. It appeared to be shut at an angle, slightly off-hinge, as if yanked from a different make of car, then reinstalled with a staple gun.

Theo stayed there, swaying, parting the blinds, wondering what Teal was doing next door. And with whom she was doing it.

the motel manager must have stopped by

Again, this seemed to be erroneous reasoning, though Theo was only willing to entertain the most convenient thoughts. The least threatening assumptions—reflections of reality that revealed Teal as his, and his alone. For keeps.

Of course it was the manager. Rent would soon be due. Teal would pay both hers and Theo's this month. Just like last month and the month before that. She would hand over dollar bills that smelled of Budweiser and BBQ sauce and lust.

Theo was looking at the limousine, seeing nothing, when the face appeared. The child's face. The face that popped up from the passenger seat, framed pale and small in the limo window. The ghost, or girl, or memory, that was suddenly there—wide-eyed, wan, and staring right back.

christ jesus

One long, soprano note sounded through the room—a keen which seemed to come from his own throat. Jerking backward, Theo tottered, hit the bed edge, toppled toward the carpet. For a moment, he experienced a sensation of suspension, a feathery buoyancy that kept him aloft, floating. But then gravity intervened, threw Theo down like a rag. The floor rose to meet him. It was dandered from decades of motel guests, gritty from years of inadequate vacuuming. It smelled like mildew and stale popcorn. Like people's tired, socked feet.

Supine, Theo didn't move. He strained to hear something, anything, beyond the confines of his room. Down the street, a car honked twice. Down the outdoor walkway, the ice machine emptied itself (as it often, spontaneously, did) spilling cold cubes like a hot slot machine.

He lay still. Fear and shiraz immobilized Theo, and he allowed both to hold him down, to flatten him against synthetic fiber and shoe grit. The child could not have been real. No more real than any other hallucination he'd hosted while intoxicated: the street lamp that became a demon; the ceiling fan that became a starfish; the thumping fucking, from the room above, that became a jungle drum. Dream often swirled into waking life. Too much drink, mixed with too little sleep, distorted Theo's vision, warped his senses like book pages dropped in bathwater.

He stayed on the carpet, crumpled as a beer can. The faucet drip-dropped. The nightstand clock tick-tocked. Minutes passed, an hour perhaps, before Teal's door opened, then closed. Theo heard man-steps. Big boot steps, heavy as hooves. They Clydesdale-clomped by his room, changing pitch when they left the covered walkway and hit the asphalt of the parking lot.

Blinking, Theo lifted his head to listen. This motion cracked his neck, made a Tilt-a-Whirl ride of the motel room. It tipped and rocked and spun. It shifted and rearranged, revolved and swayed, as maintenance man, or motel manager, or someone else altogether, walked past. The steps receded, then stopped out in the dark, out in the lot, leaving only the *clack-clack* of the heater, the rasp of Theo's uneven breathing. Already spinning, he couldn't fathom standing.

The nightstand had the shakes, and the underbelly of the bed yawed. The television yawned a blank, black screen.

On his stomach, Theo inch-wormed toward the window. Wasted as he was, the slow pace and low perspective afforded new insights, fresh observations. Beneath the bed was Ferrah's favorite toy: a pink plastic cocktail stick, a gift from Teal—the bird had been looking for that. A clump of anonymous blonde, pulled from somebody's brush, attached itself to the tufts of Theo's chest hair, as if to hitch a ride to the other side of the room. On the far face of the bureau, a foot off the carpet, the word "SLUT" had been scratched into faux walnut wood. From where he snailed, ceiling cracks took on the topography of canyons seen from space. The floor wasn't such a bad place to be. Across horizontal lines from the blinds, Theo continued to drag himself, putting one arm in front of the other, then chafing both knees forward over thick shag.

He reached the wall and paused. Panting, propped on rug burns, Theo longed to see the man, but was terrified to again glimpse the child. That small, sick face. His own daughter had been similarly fragile, a glass girl, and he never would have left her alone in a desolate lot after dark. But she didn't visit him anymore, no matter how drunk he got.

Theo palmed his way up plaster to an unsteady stand. He peeked into night. The sky was mottled with patches of silver cloud and smog, blotches of black. Far away, a car alarm echoed. The motel driveway teeter-tottered, and the lighted walkway spilled yellow onto the parking lot. Against the limousine, an enormous form hunkered, doubled over, pressing itself against the passenger door. The red door.

Theo's breath snagged in his throat. Hardly recognizable as a human figure, the silhouette straightened to a hulking height, then turned a wide girth. Before Theo could react, it moved toward the motel. Under florescent bulbs and a vacancy sign, the shape suddenly became a man. A man who ran thick hands, again and again, across jowl-scruff. A man who sagged under his own weight, who lumbered, giant as a grizzly, in Theo's direction. Pausing beneath neon, he looked back at the limo. Something held him there, fixed. His pallor was pasty. He had a face like a duffle bag.

son of bitch, she's your kid then

Standing stunned in the window, Theo was sure that, as the man turned, their eyes met. Letting the blinds snap shut, he dropped once more to the floor. Blood was hard-pumping his ears, his heart was jackhammering the carpet. As the neighboring door slammed, Theo thought of Teal with the man. Image after image flipped through his mind, as if someone were shuffling a deck of girlie cards. The contrast between their bodies would be grotesque: her curves pressed to the hairy bulk of him, her mouth open, her smooth limbs riding him like a wooly mammoth.

In a fetal position, Theo felt ill. He wanted to find his bathrobe and his deepest voice, to march next door and intervene. But some animal apprehension stopped him, some instinct of size and supremacy. That giant, with one steel-toed boot, would grind Theo out like a cigarette stub. That bloated ogre who took his Teal. That monster who'd left a little girl unattended, while he did god-knows-what with another kid, someone he no doubt considered a mere stripper.

Why was this beast granted a living, breathing child, while Theo was forever denied access to his own daughter? Why was he allowed to lock a girl, a girl the size of a shorebird, into a limo late at night? It was surely not the first time. How had he never been reported?

Theo lifted his bald spot from the carpet. Exhaling, the edges of his lips turned up.

gotcha

LUX & SADIE

"Let's limo home, huh?" Lux shouted over seagull shrieks. "What say you, Sweetness?"

Sadie pretended not to hear. Skipping on sand and stone, her arms winged wide against gusts.

Lux was beginning to feel the panic of public places, and the girl had chocolate ice cream circling her smile. Thorton Pier & Park was crowded for a Thursday. The first day, after a frozen season, of lukewarm light. Afternoon stretched shadows toward dusk. Lux watched his outline waver, long and misshapen, over pebbles. The lake was opaque, and driftwood washed in. Tide-polished, it glowed like X-rayed bone.

Their morning was spent cabbing a customer from the Blue Moon Motel, to the town strip joint, and back again. The girl deserved a moment's play. A few seconds to sprint it all out. Alders shook above the waterline where Sadie teased a duck with the latticed carcass of a waffle cone. She ran the shore, back and forth, in shorts and green goulashes, while Lux stood by the pier. Soul-sucked and world-weary. He'd received the call that morning: they wanted to take his girl.

Duck shit caked both boots. Lux licked his ice cream and felt sick. Despite April breezes, sweat wet his temples, his pits, the dips of his clavicles. Kids screamed louder from sandcastles. Breaths scratched shallower beneath his shirt.

Standing there, he knew with sudden certainty what Sadie would forget. The panacea of their palms, the fit of their hands clasped together. The rules of their games, and the grammar of their language. The *swing-creak-slam* of their porch screen. It was only natural, after all, this amnesia of childhood. Just another defense mechanism.

how the heart covers its ass

Lux's earliest memories were crosshatched and bleared at best. Sadie's landscape would surely look the same. Squint and squint as she might, he would become a distant figure, hunched and hobbling down a road that wound out of sight. A smudge, blurring into the background.

Somebody was charring briquettes. Nausea turned down Lux's mouth. Beef smoke churned his stomach. It clouded past, then rose over the horizon, wafting to nothing above soft hills.

"Sadie m' lady! Shippin' on out now!" He scanned the waterline, then spotted her, fifty tiny footprints down the shore. Working his way past the year's first, brave waders, past toddlers tipping pails, past families shivering and picnicking on plaid, he hoped his girl never felt this groveling low.

"Sadie!"

———

He was yelling from somewhere behind her.

Ducking every attempt at a tail touch, the mallard quacked ahead. Always one waddle away. Sadie giggled with frustration and exhilaration, glancing back at Lux. She would make him smile yet. This was the kind of light he liked to laugh in. But he was no longer following. His shoulders were slumping, and he was no longer calling. The hairy hulk of him stood still, staring at the lake. Strawberry ice cream dripped, pink and thick, down his shirt-sleeve.

where are you, when you look like that?

She abandoned her hunt. Lux's losses were never lost on Sadie. They found her, even when she had not called. Even when she had no name to call them. Collecting two trophy feathers, she ran to his side.

"D'you see that boy bird? Much prettier than the girls." To prove her point, she held the feathers above her head. They were lacquered dark at the quill, aquamarine where light hit.

His beard shook.

"The color's sorta the same as gas, as gasoline, you know? When it's spilled all shiny in a puddle?" She turned the feathers against the sun, awed by their iridescence.

"Let's go," said Lux, eyes fixed at a six-foot depth, where water refracted rocks and flashes of minnows.

Sadie hung on his belt buckle. It was metal, mail-ordered from Marlboro. On the steel clasp stood a horse. On the horse sat a saddle, and on the saddle was a wrangler who smoked and stared in masculine straddle. Gripping the belt, Sadie swung. She pulled Lux down to her height, down to his knees.

Crouching, Lux chin-thrust toward parking lot. "Come

on, now. Time to go."

"Stop moving all around. Lemme get you fixed and ready. For takeoff." She slid both feathers into the back of his collar, where he felt cold and damp.

When Lux stood again, she let her hand get lost in his.

———

Her palm was small, and he squeezed to find it. The feathers made his neck itch. Quill tips poked skin. With each step, Lux felt his new plumage bounce, ruffle in the wind. He knew, moving toward the limousine, that he looked like an enormous emu. People were staring, but he didn't care. He had to get off the shore. Lux had to get Sadie home.

"Why's there seagulls when there's no sea?" Snot slimed a slow trail from her nose, only to be blocked above her mouth by a splotch of chocolate cream.

Lux looked away.

"How come they're not called lakegulls, and why'd they want to leave the real ocean for here? Wasn't it far? A far ways to fly?"

Nodding, he said, "Keep moving."

"Why's those boys giving them lunch like that?'

"Sadie, Baby, let's just get back home and—" He followed her point to the pier's end. Lux stopped walking.

———

His grip tightened around her wrist. Sadie shook it free. She looked down wood planks, toward a group of boys who aimed fishing rods into the clouds. At their feet, parchment bags scattered, greased translucent from the Mr. Tasty stand (where Lux limoed on slow days for fast food). Laughter echoed across the lake. Below gyring gulls, poles bowed back, then snapped, shooting invisible lines.

Sadie pulled his arm. "Birds love those Mr. Tasty fries ...so do we, right?"

A seagull swooped from the flock, winging hookward. It screamed once, then dove—sleek and quick—snatching a fry clean from the white sky.

There were howls at the end of the pier, high fives and low jabs to torsos. Sadie looked up at Lux. Lux looked up at the boys' catch.

"Will that bird be like a fish now?"

He said nothing.

She was sure this meant something. He stood huge above her, frowning furrows into his forehead.

"How's it gonna get the hook out? Can it spit?"

———

"I said, can the bird spit?"

nah, we're fairly well snared, sweetie

Lux smiled down, "'Course seagulls can spit." She stepped onto the pier. Grabbing at coat strings, Lux drew the girl back. "Of course. What else would they do with fish bones?"

Overhead, the gull screeched, pumping hard against the line's pull. Lux was aware of appropriate action, of an onlooker's responsibility to intervene. The barb had pierced clear through the esophagus, and the bird was being lowered, tug by tug, like a flag. But he was also aware that they were still free. That it was only a matter of hours now. A matter of moments before all the difference might be made.

Stooping, Lux scooped Sadie off the ground.

———

He lifted her and squeezed. So hard, she couldn't breathe to say,

my boot

It had slipped from her sock, and lay lonely on the sand. Rubber heel to sky. Sadie squirmed in Lux's hold, as he lumbered them at a half-run to the limo. His grip pressed the air from her lungs. His pace scared her. She felt the passenger belt buckle (which he never bothered to do) and Sadie sobbed beneath it the whole drive home.

Over three speed bumps, past the tourist part of town. Along the highway and the one-lane road. Up Five Mile Hill, down the gravel drive. Through dust and their front door, she cried. For the lonesome boot. For the gull. For the man who spooned golden honey into her milk, and read to her from the bedside rocker.

Sadie let him tuck her in—snug under blue sheets. She drifted, then resisted, reluctant to leave Lux and the only room she knew. Where moths brushed against windows and her eyes fluttered at the old, wood chair. Where she watched Lux rock and rock.

LUX

Lux's earliest memory had the eerie, coppery sheen of a daguerreotype. The recollection hazed in places. It bent and distorted, bowed and warped, like light through lake water.

Lux remembered rust-colored dust rising with his own screams. A pickup truck, a dirt road, an air freshener in the shape of a pine. A man he called father, pulling from the flatbed a dog he called Fox. They had climbed miles into the hills, high above the lake, to a distance no house pet could retrace. There, sky breathed thin. Sagebrush breezed with cigarette smoke. As his father's Marlboro ashed, the country station went to static. Below, Cody County looked fit for a train set. Above, clouds looked soiled, brown. Hunkered in the truckbed, Fox howled a mournful yowl, which broke into two notes and echoed down the valley.

While the engine idled, Lux watched rough hands sink into the beloved, russet pelt. He heard the shout, "Get on now. Go!" and the sound of stones hitting the ground around the baffled animal. Fox cowered, low-moaning into the undergrowth. Lux learned, then and there, that caring can carve you clean out. That men shatter love in order to feel whole.

Standing now, in the scrap yard beside Sadie, he said, "Yup, I think it's just 'bout done."

The girl stared at the sculpture and nodded. She mimicked Lux's stance: arms akimbo, sneakers rocking, heel-toe, heel-toe.

Together, they admired their creation. It crouched, an angular creature made of metal and sharded glass. A junk dog made of lawnmower parts and reassembled memories. The work took months to construct, and the child had scoured the lot for materials. Gasket screws curved into claws. Rake prongs soldered into a ribcage, tricycle handlebars into shoulders blades. A drainpipe bent skyward to mimic the quick flick of a tail. There was movement to the beast's posture, torque to the arc of its back, to the turn of its forepaw (a radiator cap) welded midstep. The final touch was Sadie's find: two blue marbles for eyes. They were scratched from play, glinting the exact tint of the deep lake at dawn.

But Lux remembered then that Fox's stare had been brown.

hell if I got the scrap metal heart to say so

He felt his face crease into a smile (the first and only that day) as Sadie gawked at their creation. Their resurrection. Their something-from-nothing. She stared at the dog, gray eyes wide, pointer finger lodged to the knuckle up her nose.

"Sadie, Baby, for Christ's sake. You're 'bout to lose a digit."

"Was Fox a good pup? The kind that sits and fetches sticks? Like the kind that sleeps super close up and furry next to you?"

"Sure 'nuf." Lux pulled at his whiskers. They were coarse as a buffalo's, three weeks long.

Sadie pulled at her socks. They were mismatched, two different shades of beige. It was time for a new pair, but she could hold out 'til barefoot season.

where will we be by then?

Behind them, swinging from the roof's stoop, Sadie's windchime wound around itself, clanging. A rainy day art project, it clinked the same chord in succession, in shifting breezes. A broken triad, followed by a blue note. Beautiful enough to be accidental, intentional enough to be incidental. The ring of tin against wind, discordant and wrenching.

"Why'd Fox go away? Why'd he leave like that, when you were such a little boy?" She touched the dog on its soup can snout.

"Not always our choice. When to go."

"Well, he loves it here, anyways. He loves it with us."

"Yup."

Lux felt the weight of the day pressing heavy. Evening was sinking hard. Soon, along the property line, trunk-mounted lights would high-beam from trees. Bright and punctual for their night watch. Yet they'd shed little security. A visitor was coming. At an unspecified hour, on an unspecified day, a CPS representative was to arrive. For a "routine assessment, based on allegations of unsafe conditions for a child." Lux, however, had no intention of being home.

we've waited too long already

He gave Fox a pet, which sent Sadie into hysterics, then wedged his hindquarters into a lawn chair. Extended from one armrest was a rearview mirror. It reflected the scruff of his sideburn, the edge of the porch, the driveway winding gravel and weeds to Highway 5, to the wide world belonging to everyone but them.

"Nice puppy-puppy." Sadie stood eye level with the animal. She lifted a sneaker to match its stance. She showed her teeth.

Ever since the caseworker's call—when the seagull was caught, and Sadie tucked wing feathers into his shirt collar—Lux had been on edge. On too little sleep and too much weed. But he did his damndest, for the kid's sake, to keep a happy home. Bedtimes were overlooked. Rocky Road was purchased from the gas station by the frost-burned gallon. And lily white lies were told: "Nothing's wrong, Sweets, it was only a customer phoning from the bar." "Yeah, we should start a shell collection this summer." "No, Champ, my muscles're fine. Just got a kink in my neck for a sec."

But Sadie had precision in her intuition, radar in her stare. She sensed Lux's terror. She peed through three bed sheets each night and was sleep-grinding baby teeth to bone nubs.

"Think Fox'll be lonely, though? No other dogs to bark with."

Lux nodded. He readjusted the mirror.

gonna need more than a fake guard mutt to watch my back

Sadie circled the statue. "I think Fox needs a collar . . . with his name. And our phone number, case he gets lost."

"Agreed," Lux said, raising a shaking sleeve, wiping the mirror with flannel. Lux looked from Sadie to the reflection, then back again at the child—the child who wore elasticless socks, weighed less than an Easter ham, and was his one reason for living. She cupped a palm around the dog's ear, began to whisper.

that's right, give him your secrets, he won't tell

Fox wasn't the only sculpture to inhabit the scrap yard. By the road, by the CLOSED sign Lux posted that morning, two figures posed. As welcome. As warning. Hand in wrought-iron hand. The larger (by four feet) was a broad torso of sheet metal and bolts. It tilted a hubcap head. The smaller stood waist-high, wound with wire and bicycle spokes, crowned with yellow yarn that tangled in the wind. The pair rose from the same foundation, a Goodyear tire, and leaned ever so slightly into each other.

And then there was Sadie's piece.

made the autumn she was mine

On the far side of the lot, by a rickety lean-to that rotted and mossed, an old oak grew. In the cradle of its lowest branch, Lux nestled his first work of garbage art: a giant, rusted nest of twisted rebar. Created when Cal gypsied to god-knows-where, only to turn up dead. When the girl became his, and Lux became "Papa Bear." The nest was child-sized, open and jagged as jaws. It was empty of egg or chick. Full of his promise to protect.

Sadie squatted beside the dog, inspecting the iron underbelly. "Well," she said, "Fox is a boy all right."

"Feels real nice to see him again. After all this time." A cloud passed in Lux's mirror.

"Yeah, it's good to make stuff."

What Lux loved most about Sadie (aside from her galaxy of cheek freckles, her arms squeezed tight around his waist) was the kid's early appreciation of art. Its whiplash force and stand-still calm. Sadie understood healing through hurting. And she grasped the ecstasy of escape. For hours on end (the only waking hours Sadie stayed still), the girl would hover over a sheet of plywood, or paper, or metal—in the zone, alone, and miles from herself. Then came the thrill of return. The homecoming to whatever space was *here*, to whatever time was *now*—to see what she looked like when she hadn't been looking.

"Wanna throw some clay?" Sadie pointed at the dark beneath the porch where their ceramics station was stashed. On rainless days, they rigged the pottery wheel to the jacked-up limo wheel. A method invented by Lux, perfected by Sadie. While the girl burrowed below the driver's seat, pressing the gas pedal, he would call above whirling clay, "Faster . . . hold steady . . . K, slow down now . . . good, keep it there. . . ."

She sniffed. "I'll do all the spinning, though, the gas pedal part, 'cause this finger gots a band-aid."

"No pottery. Not today, Baby."

"I probably won't even make clay people then." Sadie studied her thumb. The bandage was loose, a week worn, dangling little white tassels where its edges frayed. "This might get 'fected."

"Infected," Lux corrected, kneading his neck muscles. "Something you should know, Sweets. . ."

"*In*fected," she repeated.

"Nah," Lux ran a hand through his hair, "I mean, there's something we gotta talk about."

SADIE

Sunset. The porch drenched in apricot light. BBs pinging off sheet metal, ringing clear and high. Lux's voice, husking rough and low.

"Aim to the left a bit. Hold your breath while firing."

"I *know*," Sadie whispered, winking down the wobbling barrel. She inhaled cool air and held it. Wood planks felt splintery under her bare feet, the gun heavy over her shoulder. "I know, 'cause you just said that already."

"Shhh."

Dusk always shushed their words. As if mosquitos or shadows might hear their secrets and tell. The sky made a ceiling that was far off, floating soft puffs. Sadie steadied her elbow on the railing, her stare on the target: a rectangle of thin tin halfway across the lot. The metal was as wide as she was tall, polka-dotted with bullet holes. It reflected the angle of a gable, the sea of surrounding trees, the waver of Lux's outline, pacing and piping the length of the porch. His smoke rose over them, then hovered—nowhere to go.

Sadie exhaled, re-aimed. She squinted, assessing her

projected trajectory. The target sheet glinted, soon to be the roof of their new fort. Sadie and Lux always built abodes beyond the home, hideouts around the junkyard. Caves for escape, with slanted walls, bicycle wheel windows, sandwich board doors. The metal panel would serve as a ceiling, the BB holes small dots of light—stars made of empty space. Daylight would strain through to make night. Inside, any old noontime would twinkle galaxies. Shooting constellations into the tin had been Sadie's idea. Lux liked it. He said, "Brilliant."

She pinched the trigger and the gun punched back. Hard against her cheekbone, against the tender skin beneath her eye. The bullet hit somewhere to the right of the metal, making a flat dull plunk like a coin dropped in water. Sadie fired again. The shot punctured a tire. It sighed.

"Concentrate." Lux wasn't looking at her, as if doing so might hurt. He was gnawing his pipe, wearing the day on his face like an unironed shirt.

"Sadie, pay attention."

"I *am*."

"Focus. And forget yourself, remember only that. Like when you're making art."

Sadie was nowhere near forgetting herself. Nor Lux's rifle barrel stare—at once hollowed and loaded. The stare he aimed every which way but hers. He was boot-stomping the stoop now, up and down the porch steps, in and out of her gun scope. Sadie frequently envisioned, in startling clarity, the worst conceivable situation. She often imagined the action or reaction, the cause or consequence, which would wound her most.

Sadie saw herself shoot Lux. Point-blank between his crumple in pain. Sadie saw blood on wood.

"Focus, Sweetness."

"Can't." She lowered the gun. "Papa Bear, I'm scared."

"Why, please?"

"Let's go inside now."

"All right."

———

Lux tucked Sadie in with a story. "They're all we've got," he told her. The plot Lux made up. Which is not to say it wasn't true.

He spoke slowly, evenly. Sadie breathed in and out of her mouth, slipping in and out of sleep.

". . . so then, deep in the dark dark cave, big bear and little cub lived out the rest of their lives, best they could. Because what else could they possibly do? The End." He rocked fast and hard in the chair. The wood seat creaked. Sadie felt lead-lidded, lightheaded, unsettled by the story in a way she didn't understand. But Lux's voice had lulled her. It scraped steady, sanding her smooth. She heard him stand. She felt his lips on her open, outstretched hand. She listened to him heel-toe down the long hall, as she drifted, further and further away.

———

Covered in scratchy blankets and sweat, Sadie writhed, thrashed toward consciousness. She was twisted in the damp sheets, in the oversize nightshirt, in the throes of some dream she couldn't shake. Her mother was underwater.

Calista was in the lake, moon-white and sinking. Shaking, Sadie sat upright.

The lamp was lit in Lux's room. It shed a soft glow over floorboards, a sense of calm over Sadie. Clothes piled high by the closet—his undershirts and torn jeans, her socks and tattered frocks. Books lined the wall, books she didn't understand but loved because Lux did. Because he fingered their indexes, dusted their jackets, caressed their spines like living, breathing beings. Creatures as fragile as they were powerful. A pillow had fallen onto the throw rug. It still held the impression of Lux's head.

maybe even his dream

The bed was, as always, sleep-tossed. It looked, to Sadie, like the safest place in all the world.

Lux stood staring out the window, almost swallowed by spicy-smelling pipe smoke. Rain battered the pane. His back was to her. It was pale and broad and bare. Black hairs kinked in patches across his shoulders. Sadie studied the bow of his legs, the roll of skin over his belt, and knew Lux would be hers for the rest of ever. This made her body hurt. But in a different way than when she scraped a knee, or ate too much, too fast. Sadie understood, deep in her belly, that love should feel like this. It should squeeze you, vice-tight. It should take your breath, break your bones.

Without turning, Lux said, "What's wrong, Baby? Can't sleep?"

"Bad things."

"Come 'ere."

His face was close, ragged as the coats in their thrift store. It was a face only she could hold. Sadie couldn't remember not knowing it, not adoring it. The ruts around the mouth. The dips and divots, the pockmarks that felt to her fingers like craters. Lux lifted her into his bed, covered her with worn wool. His hands were calloused and cool.

"Promise me some things, Sweetness." He nestled her against the pillows, nuzzled her neck.

A fear rose in her chest, then dropped—a BB fired skyward, then falling fast. "How many things?"

Lux paused, sucked his pipe, blew blue smoke to the ceiling. "Three," he said.

"I promise."

"Well, for fuck sake, Sweets, you haven't even heard 'em yet."

"Oh."

He pet her face, set down his pipe. "Always guard what you most need . . . guard it with all you got."

Sadie lifted one finger.

"Never, never-ever let someone else say what's best for you." He sat still, yet seemed, somehow, to be leaving. He was listening to rain.

She held two fingers in the air.

"And know, always know, when it's time. Always know when it's time to give up."

Three fingers, three promises. Sadie's arm was tired from being suspended above her head. Lux's bed felt as forgiving as sleep, his words as meaningless as printed text. She let her hand fall, her lids drop.

When Sadie woke, minutes or hours later, she knew instantly, viscerally: she was alone.

LUX

Lux loved motels: musty lobbies, olive and mustard carpets, sheets tucked tight to the mattress. Years ago—when Sadie was but a wee seed of possibility, deep in Cal's belly—he would drive for days, rudderless, just to collapse under some ragged quilt, under some roadside VACANCY sign. Motels held a nostalgia, a gut-longing he couldn't quite articulate. The wall art was always pastel (floral or pastoral), the pool chlorinated to some ungodly blue. Such lodgings stirred in Lux the urge to vanish. The desire to be swallowed by outdated décor, by curtains drawn at noon. He craved their tacky uniformity and continental breakfasts. Their legacy of threadbare sleep and suicide.

It had been pouring since morning. Fat drops that aerated lawns, made mud of yards. Rain that swelled brooks and books. Rain that became a soundscape—pattering, trickling drips at various pitches, splashing all day and into dark. The pavement was wet black, driven at this hour only by truckers, insomniacs, drunks.

or ghosts like me

The wipers were busted, and the world through Lux's windshield was an underwater swirl. Rain seeped through the crack in the glass. Headlights streamed, as shapes swam, eddied, whirled together. The limo splashed past a billboard, a cerulean moon smiling. He slowed. The Blue Moon Motel offered AC and TV (remote control not included) on the only road out of town. For a day's wage, a night's rest. At this hour, Teal would be working, far away from herself and her grimy room. But the girl would wish for him, if nothing else, at least a familiar setting. Lux swerved off the highway, following flashing arrows. The limo diagonaled across three parking spots.

here's where people come to disappear

Lit by streetlamp, his pocket watch clasped hands over XII. Last August, Sadie found the timepiece in their thrift store, in a tweed jacket he tagged at $3.99. The face was scuffed, the gold buffed by life to a burnished glow. It had been placed on Lux's pillow, tied with twine in a sad, lop-eared bow. "A merry Father's Day present," beamed Sadie. He hadn't told her the holiday had passed, now nearly ten months away.

Sitting in the parking lot, Lux listened to little ticks. Seconds, minutes, hours: gone. Sadie had gifted the one thing he couldn't give back. Gears pulsed against his palm, while Lux's time wound itself down.

didn't make a kid, but i'm 'bout to make an orphan

Beside the Blue Moon, beside himself, he dropped the watch on the dash and opened the limo door.

Lux never left Sadie home alone. More for his own lonesomeness, than for her safety.

she takes better care of herself than I can

But tonight the girl lay curled, a small ball in his bed.
Knees to chin, all 39 pounds of her in potato bug position.
Earlier that evening, Sadie sleep-wandered to stand barefoot
in his doorway. "Bad things," she said. Her hairline glistened
sweat. Her t-shirt (a tattered jersey, #2) was on backward,
nightmare-rumpled. Rain slicked the window. Leaks snaked
the ceiling. Lux had been pipe-dreaming, watching drops
race down the pane. Setting the corncob on the nightstand,
he turned to take the child in his arms, to stroke her back
toward dream.

Stepping now into midnight, he wondered what sense
Sadie would make of his absence. When dawn lifted her lids,
when Lux was gone.

I'm not worth her salt

But Sadie would cry awhile, surely. Puffy-eyed, she might
have time for Sugar Puffs in milk before the caseworker came.
She would have to pour her own. Sadie was always too
skinny in the morning. Ravenous and shivering, as if roused
from hibernation. He imagined her waking, bangs plastered
sideways, mouth smacking. All alone and Luxless. Yet for
the moment, at least, the girl was blanketed. Snoring like a
bear cub.

Through puddles and the motel entrance, Lux hunkered.
Drops clung to his beard. He sleeked them flat, shook off his
coat. The lobby doubled as a utility closet. A stale cracker
smell hung on still air. He sniffed a hint of rat poison. Tools
and brooms crowded every corner, unused in the room they
inhabited. The carpet's shag bristled grit, and the heater had
called it quits. On a table that posed as a front desk, a fake

fern posed as real. Slumped behind, in brown uniform and boredom, a man picked at his scalp.

Lux cleared his throat. *Eh-hem.* Twice.

"Oh. Sorry," the guy looked up from a porno mag. "Need directions somewheres?"

"Nah, well, not really . . . just a room. Just some space."

———

Lux's boots clomped down the outdoor corridor, past a pop machine, then an ice machine. Past slits in curtains where people screwed or stared at ceiling plaster. From a busted gutter, water gushed. It broke into streamlets against the cement, flowing toward a depression by door #4.

my door

Lux paused a few feet before. The neighboring room was flickering, blaring infomercials. Through parted drapes, he could see an empty birdcage and someone's bald spot. The television flashed, lighting the nape of the man's neck, the rock of his torso back and forth.

same sorry fucks in every motel across America

Lux sidestepped the puddle of gutter water, and tried his key. It jostled the lock, opening another memory—one that was somehow suppressed when visiting Teal. He had been to the Blue Moon once before. With Cal. With her cracked laugh, her needle by the bed, her endless sadness. With her track-mark arms around his chest, python-squeezing as she slept. Cal's grip rarely relaxed, even in dream.

even in death

Detached, floating high above himself, Lux entered the place he planned not to exit. The room was small and rectangular. The air was briny, heavy, as in the hull of a ship. A faint, burnt odor filtered from the bathroom, where a fan had been left rattling. Beside the queen-size bed, a mirror was mounted. Positioned for lovers, no doubt. It framed the mattress, the swinging bulb, the edge of his face frowning from flannel. Lux looked good in red.

matches my eyes

He sat on the mini-fridge and felt nothing—nothing but spent. Obsolete as a penny. Sadie didn't need him anymore. In fact, the girl would be better off without him. A fistful of pills, a flask full of whiskey, and she could have a happy adolescence. Parents, cardigan sweater sets, a private school perhaps. The loss of Lux might smart at first, but she would be all the healthier for it. Tougher. Flushed of his toxins, and free to host her own.

consider it a favor, baby, since you've granted me so many

Not one for ceremony, Lux took a long pull of whiskey, dropping a few blue pills into the swallow. When the swig hit his gut, he would shower. Then, dopey and ready, Lux would put on a clean undershirt, prop against the headboard, and gulp Jim Beam—bright tablets bobbing like Lucky Charms. In his hoodie pocket was a 9mm.

first gun Sadie learned to shoot with

Lifting the flask again, Lux let whiskey flow hot down his throat. Eyes closed, head back, he held her close. Sadie was his very best thought, always had been. Outside, rain drummed. Back home, a symphony of drip-drops was playing on scrap metal. The girl's stuffed animal display was, no doubt, soaked. By the front door, a baby blue slicker was hooked by its hood.

Lux stood. Mid-stumble toward the shower, something caught his glance. Across the window, sudden color. A flash against black—fragmented, rainbowed, like a quick pass through a kaleidoscope. He walked to the glass and, with one sleeve, wiped a circle. Nothing moved. Lux blinked into night, where the only moon in sight sat on a sign that read:

GOD BLESS   POOL AND CABLE TV

Then he saw it, haloed by a streetlight. Above the limousine, high on a wire, a parrot preened in the rain. Feathers riffled—green, yellow, aquamarine.

well, I'll be god-fuckin-damned

By the time he reached the cab—coat unzipped, boots unlaced—the bird was gone. Windborne for calmer skies. Lux looked back at the motel, where room 4 was left open, dim-lit against the lot. It struck Lux then, that some omens can be overlooked, passed off as simultaneity of circumstance.

and some simply can't

The edge of the motel wavered, and the pavement began to pitch. Drunk, Lux leaned against the limo. He pulled at the driver-side door. Sleepless on fifteen sleeping pills, he fell behind the wheel.

hold tight, baby, papa'll be home before you know it

———

Deep in sweet dream of Sadie, Lux twitched on the limo seat. By some twist in sleep-time, he was her same young age, walking a field of wild flowers, crisscrossing a meadowed hill. Shoeless, they waded through tall grass, hands clasped together, silhouettes hazing against the sky and the back of his eyelids.

Above a cluster of alders, the sun was setting. Beneath the pads of his feet, the planet was spinning. Spindle-limbed and giggling, the girl pulled at him. While their pace was hasty, their direction seemed uncertain. The meadow sloped, pathless. They pressed on, breathless. Switch-backing the gentle hill, holding stride beside Sadie, Lux was unsure whether they were moving away from something, or toward. Fleeing, or seeking. But he didn't care; he was with his girl.

The air felt light, rarefied—electric, and threatening thunder. Sadie wore a frock he'd never seen before, nothing from their thrift store. A shift, thin as skin (and a similar color), which billowed then clung, hugging the fine lines of her skeleton. Overhead, clouds churned. Underfoot, a softness like moss. Sadie was trying to tell him something—something of great import—yet the wind wailed as if in mourning, drowning her voice, whipping gold hair over her open mouth.

The gearshift woke Lux, pressed against his leg. With each dream step, his knee had knocked the knob. The bone cap throbbed. A bruise would be spreading beneath his jeans, blooming like wine on linen.

It was early morning, and the world was waking, renewing. An eerie, seemingly sourceless light surrounded him. Still floating, Lux pictured himself hovering, omniscient, watching the day burst wide. Everywhere, beaks opened and earthworms burrowed. Engines started and graveyard shifts ended. Puddles evaporated, too slow for the eye, mirroring a low, gray sky, a dawn like any other that would never come again. Across Cody County, lovers were parting, bacon was crisping, a woman in slippers and last night's makeup was staring at her reflection, frowning at laugh lines.

Lux smelled rain. Rain and vomit. In the battered limo, in the throes of a hangover, he tried to find his bearings. But the world was awhirl. Reality arrived in isolated images: the steering wheel, the hangnail on his pinkie, the dashboard with its odometer, dead fly, and ripped pack of smokes. These pieces remained scattered, refused to jigsaw together.

Barely awake, he smacked chapped lips. Hardly aware, he swallowed. Shame came slow and sour, a lingering after-taste, thick paste against his palette. Lux had left his girl.

sorry, Sadie, I'm so very sorry, baby

Slime coated his throat viscous. His tongue was a slug in his mouth. Memories of the motel came in flashes, in ragged patches of recollection: a gut-sinking feeling, a flask floating pills, a parrot—there, then gone.

Lux missed Cal. Abruptly, and in great surges of grief that clenched his chest, snatched his breath. He missed her fingertips, how they traced his naked back like a map, searching for a place to settle. He missed her tangles, how they smelled like lilac, and cigarettes, and sweat. Late-nights, Cal climbed the fire escape to inhale high air, to chain-smoke Chesterfields. She would perch there for hours, pale legs over open space, while he waited in bed—a hippopotamus on her slim, twin mattress. He would lie there, longing to run his tongue over her again and again, as one longs to say a poem again and again, to feel words fill the mouth, jolt the heart, tingle the spine. Cal always returned with a sigh, sliding nude and cool between sheets. Gliding a hand down the length of him, guiding Lux in. Back then, he wanted to worship the entire universe, and felt—through their fucking—that he did.

Dead lovers never leave. Even when you're half asleep. Even when you're groping out from under a hangover. They're always already present: opening windows, scratching walls, whispering never-could-have-beens. Patient, they wait in unopened books. Restless, they rustle in closets. They hijack smiles on billboards, faces on strangers, eyes on little girls. They're forever there, when you're on the brink of waking, when you're on the cusp of forgetting.

The first time he visited her apartment, it was a wreck—beer cans, bras, toddler toys, ashtrays—as if someone had tipped the studio upside down and shaken it. Calista never cleaned for him. Lux liked that. It was uncompromising, unladylike. It was take me as I am, or to hell with you.

Cal's absence sat beside him now, a presence in the empty passenger seat. Lux moaned. His head lolled onto the wheel, causing a long goose honk. The sound echoed over asphalt, over basalt hills, cobalt in dawn light. It jarred him alert. He jiggled the key, then the stick, stuck in neutral.

fuck

He briefly considered the term, neutral. It struck Lux, through dusky consciousness, as a lewd word. Its sound. The way it made a sphincter-pucker of his lips, an ewww noise of his voice. Not to mention its meaninglessness.

nothing in life is neutral

He gripped ten and two, unsure of what to do. Through unknown hours, the engine had idled with Lux. Now the dashboard was dark, the motor dead. Beyond the windshield and its cracked glass, dawn broke in streaks, in splatters the color of bathwater. He squinted. Sight hurt. Vision, involuntary and sudden, made his sockets ache. Lux rubbed at eye grit, blinked at dank light.

Past the front fender, a quail family cooed, single-file into a bush. Leaves shook, tear-dropping dew. Shapes shadowed, shifting purple against earth. A road he had no recollection of travelling stretched straight and trafficless, tapering to a point below a far-off oak. On the horizon, an old barn slumped. Lux had no idea where he was, but knew, by the tilt of his seat, that the tires were in a rut. The treads had been worn bare, years ago.

impossible, even with a working engine

Everywhere, the ground was mud. Sometime during the night, the rain had stopped, and the landscape—fields, hay bales, a lone prowling cat—seemed sodden, weighed down with wet.

Sadie would still be asleep, lips slack, nightshirt twisted. Lax in Lux's bed, an hour away from her clockwork waking. He had to get back. The scrap yard was coming alive without him—fuzzy bees in high weeds, light on metal, girl-snores by a comforter kicked from the sheets. Soon, caseworkers would climb the porch steps with clipboards. They would stand before the front door and knock. They would find it unlocked.

Lux tried the ignition again, then sat and watched the cat. It was brindled black and beige, with dreadlocks clumping along a swinging, sagging underbelly. She had teats like turkey basters. Her spine showed, a ridge of bumps running neck to haunch.

poor thing, probably has a shit-ton of kittens

There was a sleepy resignation to her hunt, a why-the-hell-bother posture. Snout low, tail tucked, she picked through dew, pecking drowsily like a bird too late for worms. Rolling down the window, Lux breathed deep. His face in the side mirror was ashen as morning, haggard as evening. He met his own eyes, webbed with red, and felt no recognition.

Several yards away, weeds rustled. The cat paused, one paw pointing. Her ears perked—two pert triangles—then fell back, flat and mad. Lux hoped she'd nab a quail. Her pelt bristled. With new ferocity, she hissed, lunging at some prey he couldn't see. Screeches rose where grass parted and shook.

Out of the thistle leapt a rat-sized cat, a kitten, bright white and mewing. The fur, so vivid on dark soil, startled Lux. The small body seemed to bounce, rather than run, its coat the same color and puff as a Q-Tip. If the other animal were the mother, she showed no nature to nurture, no instinct to protect. In fact, she began to bat at the baby, mouth wide with fangs. The kitty squeaked back, only to be slashed across the flank. Slinking low by the limo, warning growls gurred from the larger cat. She glanced around, glare slitted yellow, and skulked away, leaving pawprints in mud.

When the kitten turned to follow, Lux saw why it had been rejected. He looked at the pipe-cleaner tail, the tiny face cocked with curiosity. One pink eye blinked pitifully up at him. Where the second should have been, a crinkle of skin and scar tissue massed like raw hamburger meat. Lux stared, feeling a confusion of revulsion and compassion.

creepy little freak, aren'tcha?

With a jolt of guilt, he thought of Sadie—left behind by Cal, abandoned by Lux. He felt bile rise his in throat, acidic against his esophagus. Opening the limo door, Lux swung both legs into morning. He stood, cold-sweating, swaying, and would have tipped were it not for ankle-deep muck sucking him into the earth. The kitten made a high-pitch whine, like the mouth of a balloon pulled wide. It quivered all over, white paws dark with dirt. The cyclops eye closed, then opened again, fixed on Lux.

"Come'ere, you."

Without knowing why, he moved toward it, clicking his tongue. Each step made a kissing sound, as his boot heels squished through sludge. Minutes—and several mud-slips later—the kitten sat weightless on his palm, purring vibrations down his wrist. Making revving sounds like a small motor.

Lux looked around. The sky was white now, gauzed over, with splotches of light seeping through. No one drove the road, which by Lux's best guess, ran east to west. Probably miles from the lake, from the junkyard and his dreaming child.

not much to do but walk

So he did, pushing the kitty into the pocket of his hoodie. The chosen direction, left and maybe west, was arbitrary. Down the side of the road, where cement met dirt, Lux lumbered along. The cat turned a tight circle in the dark, then settled. Snug in its pouch. A little tongue licked Lux's hand. He flicked back at it, thumb cocked and ready for the first car that passed.

FAYE

Stealing the mannequin wouldn't be easy. It would require planning, maneuvering. A sly, feline slinking to which Faye was unaccustomed. She plotted every possibility, allowed for every hypothetical: where to hide if interrupted, what to say if spotted, how to explain the mannequin's absence if asked.

In the days leading up to the abduction, Faye avoided the window display at Daryl's Department store, the arrangement of mannequins who wore featureless faces and next season's styles. She tried to meet coworkers' eyes, appease customers' complaints: "This skirt didn't fit right;" "Whadya mean briefs can't be returned?" Faye's hands shook, five shifts straight. Her jaw clenched, night after sleepless night. She gnawed her nails until they bled. Dr. Nelson upped her Xanax, then the pharmacist recommended a different cocktail altogether. Cody County's sole sleep specialist increased her intake of pink insomnia pills. By the day of the robbery, Faye was ready to bring the mannequin home.

The most she had taken, in sixty-six years, was a vow of marriage, a bow at a piano recital, and a categorical exception to dishonesty. Now this: a life-size, plastic man. But it would be worthwhile. He would protect her, keep her safe. Of course, Faye made sure to dress him first, in a button-down oxford, a tight-knit sweater vest, a pair of pleated khakis. His socks were calf-length and wool. It was still chilly out, after all.

Their exit—hand in polystyrene hand, wrinkled arm around navelless waist—required coordination. Faye's workday ended at seven, an inconvenient time to take a fake person. There was the security guard to consider. There was Regina, who worked late in lingerie. There was the brisk walk across the parking lot, past Lonnie's salon, where stylists might still be sweeping up split-ends and nail clippings. For these reasons, for the fear she invariably felt at nightfall, Faye opted for an early morning mission. On Sunday, Daryl's didn't open 'til eleven. On Sunday, Faye unlocked the employee entrance under the pretext of a forgotten purse. On Sunday, she stole for the first time in her life.

It felt good.

Shadowed and chilled, Daryl's at dawn had the allure of an empty museum. Display cases winked metallic containers—compacts and lipsticks slick and lacquered as jewels. Moving through the store, Faye tingled with a sort of reverence, a white-knuckled awe she never experienced on shift. Her pupils dilated. Her pumps made church-nave echoes over tile.

As she approached the display, the sun crested Lonnie's Salon, spilling gold in dust-moted shafts. Faye's mannequin posed for the ensuing summer. He stood in the window's glow, in Bermuda shorts, in a lazy-beach-day posture: pelvis at a virile angle, head cocked at some sunny horizon. On the floor beside him was a towel, a snorkel mask, a cooler (filled, no doubt, with baloney sandwiches and O'Doul's). The figure was surrounded by family: a woman mannequin, bald and svelte in a black one-piece; a girl mannequin, plastic-pigtailed and seated with sand toys; and a boy mannequin, whom Faye imagined would have freckles and dimples. Had he actual skin, that is. The man's loved ones seemed to watch as she dragged him from the shore, from their constant, silent company.

"Let's get you dressed and home."

Past the salon window, with its line of hairdryers like astronaut helmets, Faye pretended the mannequin was her date. Just in case the manicurist was early to work. Just in case the owner was doing payroll, or the morning janitor was cleaning sink basins. She held him upright and gentleman-like, gliding chivalrously beside her, an inch off the sidewalk. When his hand slipped to the curve of her haunch, she straightened him with a hip-check.

oh no you don't, mister

It hadn't occurred to Faye that the mannequin wouldn't fit in her Buick. That she would have to slide his hairless head against the car ceiling, wedge his knees against the dash, bend his midsection 'til it made a dull, hollow crack. The man was an ideal, a model form onto which shoppers projected fantasies and insecurities. But Buicks were not built for ideals. When three fingers snapped off with the door's slam, it was almost too much for Faye to take. She gasped as one rolled, irretrievable, beneath the car. Grasping after it, her knee scraped asphalt. A long, oval hole tore through her nylons, down the length of her shin. Faye collected a ring finger and a pinkie from the pavement, put them into her cardigan pocket, then rounded the Buick to tremble behind the wheel.

She started the engine and apologized to the mannequin. He sat staring out the windshield, raising his hand to show a thumb, a pointer finger, and three, uneven stubs.

"Sorry. Truly." Setting the detached digits on his lap, she gave his leg a pat. "Though there's little need for the middle one, really. What with your line of work."

He said nothing.

Together, they took a circuitous route toward her apartment. A detour through dawn and the outskirts of town. A lupine and aspen-lined loop around the lake's south shore, up into hills the color of bruised fruit. This time of year, morning turned the mountains alizarin, the knolls surrounding Cody County a brooding mauve. The air smelled rinsed. Apple trees shook limbs in the wind. Their twigs were just beginning to bud, to split at the tips with fuzzy green nubs.

Daybreak seemed to Faye (and perhaps even to the mannequin) like a simulation of the nascent season. Sunrise seemed a microcosm of spring. Everything was possible, alive, about to be. All was bright and beginning. They missed the turn to her apartment, pressing on past orchards, haystacks, fields with lily-padded ponds, wild rye, and stubby, bleating goats. Faye felt high—on her first steal, on her newfound security, on the morning unfolding before her. A chattering of starlings crossed the sky, and the massive dosage of medications never crossed her mind.

Sitting next to the mannequin, gripping the steering wheel with one hand, the plastic of his kneecap with the other, Faye knew she'd made the right move. He would not be missed from Daryl's. People were no longer appreciated these days, no longer acknowledged. But he would be noticed, by potential intruders, in her apartment window. His shape would be seen from the street—standing guard, posing strong. She planned to move the mannequin every few hours, from one window to the next, from one stance to another. She would slacken the curtain sash, so his outline loomed in silhouette. She would akimbo his elbows, jut his jaw, so he appeared vigilant, guardant.

When her husband died, ten years earlier, Faye experienced a naked freedom. She was emancipated. She was exposed. Paul's presence had been a wool pullover—warm, utilitarian, chafing. Without him, life was stripped bare, unbounded, bearable only through routine. Only through the regimented management of minutes and activities: clocking in and out of Daryl's, clipping coupons and crock-pot recipes, counting calories and sheep. Faye had been fine, for a time. But then fear broke into her apartment while she was away at work. It entered through slats in heat ducts, cracks in baseboards, gaps beneath doors. It waited on the telephone line, on the five o'clock news, on Faye to fall asleep. It was a heart attack stat, a terrorist plot, an investment scam. When reports of the House-Sit Bandit started to circulate, Faye knew she was far from safe.

She took a curve too fast and the mannequin tipped in his seat. Righting him, she said, "The apartment'll suit you, I think. It's not Daryl's, but you can see children playing, and people walking, and chimneys smoking, and—on a clear day—the park far off." By the slight bow of his head, she could tell that he was listening, that this idea appealed to him.

They continued to wind farther from town, from street signs, stoplights, and familiar terrain. They passed hobby farms with cobby ponies, lone silos with rusted tractors. They spoke few words, and Faye was happy to drive on with the mannequin by her side. She didn't know where they were, or where they were going. She didn't care. She was no longer alone.

The road narrowed, switch-backed higher and higher into hills. Pavement turned to gravel, gravel turned to dirt. Pines took the place of aspens; sagebrush took the place of pines. The lake disappeared from view then reappeared as a puddle. Turns hairpinned, one after another, listing the Buick like a lifeboat. Yesterday's rain had made mud of the one lane. The car slid, right then left, through sludge. When Faye swung the wheel and pumped the brake, the man's severed fingers rolled off his lap and onto the floor mat.

"Now don't go losing those," she said, stretching toward the digits, straining to keep her head above the dashboard, her eyes above the glovebox. The car swerved and shimmied, side-skidding several feet, sending up puffs of dust like smoke signals. In an attempt to recenter, Faye overcorrected, veered to the opposite shoulder where shrubs bumpered an abrupt embankment. The mannequin tilted 'til his temple was an inch from Faye's face, his dismembered hand reaching out to grab hold of the wheel.

What she saw next, rounding a tight turn, fighting to

regain control of the car, caused her to shriek and stomp the brake like someone flattening a spider.

good god

A man was walking the road alone. Against wind and all reason. Faye's purse launched off the backseat with a leather slap. Her mannequin fell forward. On rain-muck and rock, the Buick glided. Tire treads slid. Time slowed. Feet from the front fender, wearing a tattered sweatshirt and a near-beard, the man raised both hands in surprise. He clutched something bright. For what seemed a small eternity, Faye held his stare.

While the seatbelt locked, pressed against her blouse and breast, took her breath, she studied the shock on his face, the bags beneath his eyes. While the wheels spun, Faye realized she recognized him. The car fishtailed, angled perpendicular to the road, then stopped. Faye heard stones, dislodged by the back tires, bounce down the hillside to find new permanence. She heard her own pulse, bloodrushing her ears. She saw the kitten.

It hung from the man's hand, mouse-size, striking white. The paws were tiny, each pad no bigger than a baby's pinkie. They pointed stiffly at the hood of the car, as if to cushion collision. Mud caked its miniature legs, whiskers waved in the wind. The color of the kitten's fur mesmerized Faye, who sat motionless, pressing the brake pedal with her entire weight. Its coat all but glowed. She stared at the snowy underbelly, the scrawny tail dangling down like a piece of twine. When she focused on the cat's face, Faye felt faint. She blinked. It winked back with one, coral-colored eye. For a moment, Faye forgot about both the mannequin and the man. All she saw was the mass of reddish tissue where the kitten's second eye should have been. All she felt was fear.

With the sudden stop, her mannequin had face-planted into the radio dial. He seemed to be listening for distant frequencies. Beyond the windshield, the man stood stunned, still holding the cat outstretched—as if its small, mangled mug might thwart impact. Across the eye socket, crimson skin wrinkled. It was crinkled, corrugated, scrunched into folds of flesh.

Faye stared. She had no clue what to do, so she did nothing. It was up to the man. Or the mannequin. Or the kitten.

The kitten made the first move, squirming, swinging on white scruff until the man shoved it into his pocket like a handkerchief. As he started toward the car, a spasm of panic seized Faye. She fumbled for the door lock, but accidentally cracked her window instead. A mewing was coming from his sweatshirt, a squishing sound from his boots.

where have I seen you?

It was the guy's voice, rumbly as a rock tumbler, which enabled Faye to place him.

"You okay, lady?"

She put the car in park, let out a long breath. He had that store and that strange little girl. In the weeks since she bought the lamp, Faye thought of the child often. She had intended to investigate the situation, perhaps even notify authorities about questionable living conditions, but Faye's own issues intervened. The loneliness. The sleeplessness. The House-Sit Bandit, and the sense of security he stole from her.

"Ma'am, you all right?" She could tell he didn't recognize her.

"Yes, yes, fine," Faye said through the window. Feeling foolish, she lowered the glass the rest of the way. This man had given her the mattress, the mattress that brought comfort. This man had a kid and a kitten. While his ability to care for either was debatable, he was no killer. Nor was he the House-Sit Bandit, as he already had a house. It was rotting, mossing, flaking ancient paint. It was gabled and triangled, with a porch, a junkyard, and boxer shorts blowing on a sagging line.

"Any chance I can get a ride back toward town? Car broke down."

lord almighty, what a face, a wonder he just walks around with it

It was a weather-beaten face, cliff-craggy, as if carved by great glaciers, worn away by erosion. It was a face on which one could trace the passage of time, the ravage of wants and aches. His skin seemed composed of compressed layers, small stones pounded into a solid surface.

macadamized

"Actually, I'm going this way." Faye pointed up the mud road, which wound around and around the hill to hell-if-she-knew-where.

"Been walking. A real long time. I'd sure appreciate a lift."

The words made his cheeks jiggle like hound dog jowls. She'd forgotten the shocking width of his nostrils, the breadth of his shoulders, the depth of his pockmarks.

adolescent acne . . . tragic, really

The man was frowning at the mannequin. Faye looked

from one to the other, as if considering an introduction.

"Well, see the thing is—"

"Not even all the way to town, just to the main road." His eye-whites were veined, a webwork of broken blood vessels. His hair grew spare around the forehead, ruddy around the mouth.

"Well, actually, I . . . um, *we* . . ." Faye nodded at the passenger seat, "were headed the opposite direction." She straightened in her seat, proud-planting a palm on the steering wheel.

The man glanced again at the mannequin. "Taking the carpool lane?"

"No. I mean . . . no, it's just that this isn't the best time—"

"Listen, my daughter, my little girl's at home. All alone." A tiny paw poked from his pocket. It batted at the string of his sweatshirt. "Please."

After seeing their house, their anything-goes life, Faye wasn't surprised the child had been left unattended. He'd been away overnight, from the looks of it. As a rule, she never picked up hitchhikers, but the responsibility to help was staring her down. It was up to Faye. Faye and her mannequin. If an intervention were indeed necessary, this visit would provide an opportunity to assess the situation. The girl needed her. Faye needed that.

"I guess so. If you don't mind sitting in the. . ."

The man was already opening the car door, cramming his bulk into the backseat.

"Many thanks."

Jerking the Buick forward, then in reverse, Faye managed

to turn around on the narrow road and retrace her tracks. Behind pines, the sky was overcast—a great bowl of clouds, curded as cottage cheese. They drove in silence, save for the sound of wheels through sludge. She was wordless, appreciating the mannequin's presence more than ever. To be alone with the man would have been beyond awkward. He smelled sour, like liquor spilled on an unwashed undershirt. Like sweat on skin and no sleep. She struggled toward small talk.

"Rain finally stopped."

"Sure 'nuf," he said. Faye heard shifting in the seat behind her.

"Bet we're in store for more soon, though." She wondered where her purse had fallen and glanced in the rearview mirror. Their eyes met. Faye looked away.

"So . . . how old's your daughter?"

The kitten squeaked once and was quiet.

Faye continued, "So, guess there's talk of a new grade school being built. But I'm sure you knew that already. So." She let out a nervous laugh. "Hard to get anything done 'round here, though. Your kid'll probably be graduated by that time."

"Pull over."

"What?" She tapped the brake, assuming some obstacle lay before them—a rock, or a woodchuck. Then Faye felt hot breath on her neck, cold metal pressed against her temple.

"Pull over. Pull over, now."

STERLING

they must've spent 50 grand, just on their can

Sterling considered this, forehead to forearm, ass to artisan tile. Under the shower's downpour, he sat, deep breathing. Water was always calming. He watched the drain swallow the day's dirt: sweat and grit and sadness. Drops pelted, hard as hail. They hammered his back, matted his hair, pooled around his toes. The stall was encased in glass, save for one wall, where tiles mosaiced into the image of a mermaid. She smiled down at Sterling. The shower was a designer model, the kind featured in fancy hotels and glossy magazines. It was the size of most kitchens. It shot hot from four, high-mounted nozzles, each pressure-fit for a fire hose.

lucky if I leave with any skin at all

An hour before, he'd entered the house via the dog door—a rectangular aperture cut for a small Collie, maybe a large Labradoodle. Sterling had always been scrawny, adolescent-shaped his whole adulthood. All angles, skin pulled thin over bone. Squirming on one side, he had no trouble squeezing through the opening, pushing past the swinging flap, and into the basement. There he stood still, holding his breath and a doggy treat, anticipating the patter of approaching paws, the low rumble of growls.

But none had come. And none would come, 'til tourism rose with the temperature. 'Til rain levels fell. It was clear, from the home's overgrown grass and unswept walkways, that the residence was only occupied during summer—which was the case with most lake-lining properties. Sterling had stayed in many. Over the preceding weeks, he'd learned to make himself liquid, to seep through spaces homeowners assessed as impassible.

All his life, people had seen Sterling (if they saw him at all) as bland, blendable. Insubstantial and somehow bendable. He shared this opinion, and his body seemed to agree, growing into itself accordingly. A sallow, unmemorable face allowed him to merge into crowds unnoticed. A narrow, flexible figure allowed him to wedge through cracks, contort through gaps. Locks were a bobby pin click to pick. Fake rocks were never more than a yard from the front door. Keys glinted in flower pots, greeted him beneath welcome mats. The ease with which he moved around Cody, from one address to the next, still shocked him.

Sitting now, under the shower's powerful stream, Sterling was as grateful as he was exhausted. This house was spacious, luxurious, all his. At least for an evening or two. A mini-mansion, equipped with cable television and a well-stocked kitchen. (He'd checked both before climbing the stairs.) Even the soap lather was lavish, a rich lavender cream. It scented the steam, and had, a moment earlier, lubed his palm for a short spurt down the drain. New surroundings always aroused Sterling, awoke his vigor, blasted lust like stardust through his veins.

But the day's wandering had left him wobbly, weak, so he shampooed from a fetal position, from a bottle of Herbal Infusions For Her. Bubbles sudded, then rinsed away. The directions read, *Repeat.* So he did, while eyeing the mosaic, the deformed mermaid flirting from a conch. Her tail was gray tile, scaled with green. Covering two rounds of breast, yellow hair coiled. Turned in profile, her face showed both thick-lashed lids, both nostril dots, rendering the work Picassoesque in a way that was clearly accidental. In fat hands, she cupped a seashell. From crown to fin, the mergirl stretched the length of the stall.

what would possess someone to pay for that?

Reaching up, he replaced the shampoo on the shower shelf, adjusting the label to the exact angle at which it was found. Most people, Sterling was certain, never knew he had stopped by for a visit.

Since being fired from Horizon Home, since his purpose was taken with his nametag, days were passed crouching. In bushes, in orchards, in abandoned barns. Or, if lucky, in posh vacation homes, with lawns sloping toward groomed shores and private docks. Yet even when he found such accommodations, when he discovered hide-a-keys or unlocked screens, Sterling was jumpy. On edge and high alert. He would only cross rooms at a crawl, creeping below windows. He would only raid pantries at night, behind closed blinds and darkness.

Once, while Sterling was filling a whirlpool tub with bubbles, the doorbell rang. This led to his hiding in the closet, in the folds of a fur coat for four hours. Last week, while standing in borrowed bedroom slippers, sniffing at a package of cold cuts, a cleaning lady entered and screamed. This led to his throwing honey ham at the woman, then running down the street in rain and fuzzy bunny feet. Neither interruption, as far as Sterling knew, led to his identification. The acquaintances he'd made (a few coworkers from Bright Horizons, a bank clerk, a landlord) thought he left town. If word of break-ins circulated Cody County, Sterling would be the least likely suspect. People would sooner imagine their own grannies contorting through dog doors. Not staid Sterling, boring Sterling. Predictable Sterling, who had never missed a shift, a shave, a rent payment. Weak Sterling, whose voice trembled in front of women, whose hands fumbled in front of men.

Sterling stood in the stall, knees wobbling like a day-old fawn. He slicked his hair and swung open the glass, releasing heat, billowing steam. The towel rack was a tiered pyramid beside the shower, bars draped with plush cloth. Before drying, Sterling memorized how the fabric had been folded: lengthwise, widthwise, then doubled lengthwise again. This attention to detail could make or break a break-in. These precautions mattered. In careful trespassing, he took pride. From the metal rack, he took a towel. It was sage color, beach-mat size, smelling of fabric softener and seven-figure incomes. Togaed in terrycloth, Sterling made his way down a long hall to the master bedroom.

In the unlit space, objects made strange shapes: the bulge of a bureau, the squat of an ottoman, the abyss of a king-size bed like a chasm in the center of the room. Outside, darkness covered Cody County. The lake was sequined, metallic under the moon. Homes glowed with residents settling in for the evening, with people cooking, reading magazines, staring at television screens, unseeing. Their windows were reflected on water, a string of holiday lights. Sterling felt cozy, drowsy, part of a human community preparing for the nothingness of sleep. For a night indistinguishable from any other, and never to be remembered.

When visiting homes that were not his own, bedtime held no promise of slumber. No guarantee of clean sheet or comforter, of feeling snuggled or swaddled. Tucking-in typically meant that Sterling would sprawl on top of the bedspread to shiver beneath a towel. This was a matter of safety, of remaining alert, ready to bolt. It was also a matter of breaking and entering—of dreaming and waking—undetected. Rich women always remembered how they'd made their beds (if they did, indeed, make their own beds). The fewer times his stay was noted, the better.

But on this night, his intrusion would go uninterrupted. The property was a vacation home, no doubt about it. Without snow sports or warm weather, visitors rarely came to Cody. What city-dweller would brave mountain passes to entertain more rain? What tourist would bungalow away a wet spring in a summer house? Lakewater was cold, unswimmable. Side roads were muddied, barely drivable. Tonight, this space belonged to Sterling. He dropped the towel, pulled back the quilt, and climbed nude into bed.

just for a few hours, then food

Sighing, Sterling felt secure in the fact that docks and buoys were boatless, beaches bare, bars filled only with local drunks whom years had slayed. Kids who found themselves suddenly trailer-parked and fifty. All grown up and beaten down. Middle-aged men who sat on the same barstools, slept in the same beds, screwed the same women whom they'd learned to despise and forgot how to live without.

There came, then, a twisted satisfaction in his own good fortune, in other people's despair. For the first time since being fired, Sterling felt glad for what he had: the luxury of king-size sheets, the ability to move about freely, the liberty of a new life stretching out before him like a wide country road.

yes, reinvention is possible, you can start over

The room was warm, the mattress a perfect softness. Whenever Sterling started to ebb toward sleep, a liquid weightlessness lifted him, floated and eased him. These sensations he'd always understood as womb-memories. They returned Sterling to a security and a sanctuary, lost long ago. He welcomed them, freed from gravity, then from reality.

———

What woke Sterling was not a sound, but a feeling. A sense of a presence. He blinked into black, straining through sleep's residual sheath. All he heard was the bedside clock, two tocks slower than the tick of his own pulse. All he saw was the angle of the open door, the arch of the armchair, the length of his body—blanketed by moonglade off the lake. Fear fixed Sterling to the pillow. Panic flattened him. His breaths came ragged, snagging in his esophagus. He tried to hold them in, which only made him gulp air like a beached sea bass.

a dream, just a dream

Yet Sterling didn't remember dreaming anything. Only sinking, deeper and deeper, into warm pools of slumber. Then terror, the certainty that someone had come home. But the house was quiet. Branches braided shadows along the wall. Wind shivered twigs, shook limbs back and forth, scrawling a strange calligraphy on plaster. Sterling talked himself out of helpless paralysis, then out of bed. He stood naked at the window—goosebumped and disoriented—still trying to shake sleep, the belief that something had jarred him awake. On the lake, a lone boat cut through night, flashing a red light. It blinked at uneven intervals. The water shimmered silver, the house remained silent.

With sudden urgency, Sterling realized he was starving. His last meal had been two days ago, something casserolesque, stolen from a kitchen a block away from where he now stood. Fear subsiding, gut growling, Sterling turned from the window.

bet this place has frozen steak, that fancy, kobe kind

Just as he bent to pick up his towel, as he began to imagine the smell of searing meat, a door slammed downstairs. Before Sterling could move, the bedroom light flipped on, blinding bright. He threw out one hand, as if to thwart an attack, covering his crotch with the other. In the doorway stood a small, red-headed boy who wore striped pajamas, rubber boots, and a stare.

For a moment, each watched the other, neither moving.

Then the child said, "Oh . . . sorry," turned in his galoshes, and walked away.

A woman's voice yelled from downstairs, "Sam? Sammy,

take off those dirty shoes before running everywhere! Not another step!"

Shaking, Sterling rushed to the window. A fifteen-foot drop. Mud, garden stones, shrubs—a hazardous jump. Not until he undid the latch, slid open the pane, felt night wind on skin, did Sterling remember his nakedness, his clothes in the bathroom at the end of the hall. A clatter echoed up the stairs. A boy's laugh, a cupboard's bang, a woman's chatter.

oh jesus

He scanned the room, considering hiding. The space beneath the bed was a mere four inches, carpet to box-spring. The closet was an empty enclosure, void of laundry bins or coats behind which to crouch. Hair pricked on his bare arms. Frozen and exposed, Sterling's nudity heightened his vulnerability. Hurrying to the bureau, pulling one knob after another, he saw at last, deep in the bottom drawer, a rumple of cloth. He grabbed at floral print. It unfolded into a long, daisy-dotted nightie.

One floor below, footsteps sounded on tile.

Tugging the nightgown over his head, Sterling hurried back to the window. He stared down. A drizzle breezed into the room. It wet his face, wafted the fragrance of spring, of new growth pushing through soil and shadow.

The woman's nags came again, this time from the second floor. "It's late, Sam, let's get your teeth brushed. Come on. Upstairs. Now."

Sterling looked from the doorway, to the ground below the window. He climbed onto the sill. His nightgown billowed.

"Bring your bag up, too. It's by the sofa." Her voice was

mom-tired and right outside the room.

"No," called the child, "no, I won't. 'Cause there's a man up there."

"What?!"

Sterling didn't wait for the boy's response. Barefoot and terrified, he leapt into black. The fall was short, just long enough for his stomach to rollercoaster to his throat. Bushes came at him, thorny and fast, and wet earth did little to cushion impact. With a mud-thud and a groan, Sterling landed. Bolts of shock and pain shot up his legs. Branches scraped his arms, ripped the hem of his flowered gown. Sterling had tried to loosen every limb for landing, to tuck into a ball on the ground, but the bushes crumbled him at an angle. His left ankle made a crack and ached. On hands and knees, Sterling pulled himself out of undergrowth. As he wobbled upright and began to hobble across the garden, he heard the woman from the window above.

"Hey!"

Sterling broke into a lurching run across the lawn, around the house, down the driveway, into the dark. It was not until he had scaled three fences, limped past several swimming pools, tripped over endless driftwood, and thrown himself, face down, by the lake's edge, that Sterling remembered the boy. The shock on his face. The mud on his boots. The innocent, "Oh, sorry," when he turned on the light and saw Sterling. For several minutes after returning downstairs, the kid didn't even think to mention an intruder to his mother.

he apologized to me . . . what purity

Sterling wanted to go back to the house, to take the

child in his arms, to tell him that he was a good boy, that time would betray them both, that things would never again be so simple and intricate. So pure and complex.

It was raining harder now, plump drops that splashed on Sterling's neck. Blood covered his face and arms. It dripped from countless scratches, running warm, thinning with falling water. He lay on his stomach on the sand. There was no moon. It, too, had fled. Sterling tucked his legs up inside the nightie, held himself in a hug, and sobbed.

SADIE

She'd searched the entire junkyard. Even though the limo wasn't in the driveway, and his bootprints stopped at tire tracks. Even though the hall clock bonged twelve times, and the lot was black. She knew Lux was gone, but Sadie searched anyway. Under the porch, behind the lean-to, through the labyrinth of scrap, in all three of their forts. Wearing a knee-length t-shirt and untied sneakers, she looked and looked. Lux had never left her before. His absence pressed her chest, knotted her gut. She yelled, *Papa Bear*, again and again, through doubt and pounding rain. Through tears and night.

Sadie was sure she'd done something wrong. Lux knew her secrets. He knew the naughty things she did, often before she did them. He had, no doubt, found out about the pretty red pen she pocketed at the drug store. Or the milk she drank straight from the carton.

or the imagining I did about the gun

Sadie was bad. So Lux left. Back inside, she'd wandered from room to room, then collapsed in his bedside chair. Her face wanted to keep crying, but it ran out of water. It scrunched and twisted, trying to wring out more wet. Sitting in his rocker, shivering all over, she wondered where he went. When a customer called late for a cab, Lux would always carry her to sleep in the limo's backseat. When he needed more stinky drink or pipe smoke, she would accompany him to the store, or to the bald man's garden room.

Wherever Lux had gone, Sadie knew it was for good.

The sun wasn't ready to wake up yet. This time of year, it slept in. But since she returned to the house, the sky had softened. It was gray around the edges now, hammering raindrops like nails, battering the windowpane with patters at alternating pitches. Sadie couldn't stop shaking. Her nightshirt was soaked from hours searching. It clung to her stomach, stuck to the back of the chair. She rocked hard and fast, like Lux would when he was worried. The wood legs whined, the floorboards creaked.

come home, come home

To the rhythm of these words, Sadie rocked back and forth. She squeezed her eyes shut, tried to hear the sound of the front door, of boots walking the hallway, of her name spoken as only he could say it. With the urgency of fear. With the tender pleading of prayer. *Sadie baby, Sadie m' lady.* On the back of her lids, she saw Lux step into the room. She saw his wide smile, his barrel belly, his hand reaching out to tussle her hair. Sadie inhaled. She smelled pipe puffs, armpit sweat, sweet rain carried in from outside.

come home, come home

Rocking calmed her. Or, rather, it provided an outlet for her anxiety, a kinetic conduit for her dread. Deep down, below her nightshirt, below her heart that hurt, she knew he was dead. Not dead like her mother, but dead for always. Sadie breathed with the cadence of the chair against floor-boards, with her chant against silence. She began to float. At a frantic pace, she pitched to and fro, drifting from the room, from exhaustion, to memories she'd not hosted for years—if ever. These had remained gauze-wrapped, pristine, untainted by repeated review: Cal swinging her around and around by the arms in an empty parking lot; Lux sleeping on the front porch, still biting a pipe, their first summer in the scrap yard; a toddler's-eye-view of the dinner table, her mother standing suddenly, planting a punch plumb where Lux's ear met his beard—blood on the rug.

Sadie moved, back and forth, in measured time, some-how outside of time. Days passed, or seconds. When wheels crunched gravel outside, she leapt from the chair, unaware of how long she'd rocked. Morning was mottled on the window. A dirty light made the sky beige, her arms a sick yellow. She ran to the sill.

"Papa Bear!"

But Lux's car had changed shape. Slow-rolling down the driveway was not a rusted limo with busted fenders and one red door, but a van she'd never seen before. It was tan, with looping writing Sadie couldn't read. She ducked from view, peeked above the window ledge. A man was driving. A woman sat beside him, pointing toward the front porch. Sadie intuited, with instantaneous certainty, that they were here for her. That Lux was no longer, and that these people had come to tell her so.

Turning, her elbow knocked the chair into motion. It ghost-rocked as she rushed from the bedroom, down the hallway, through the kitchen, out the back door. The rain had stopped, and the scrap yard was mud. Moving through it was like wading through deep water, or deeper dream. Sadie tripped twice on loose laces, and was vaguely aware that her knee was bleeding. It felt wet, warm, trickling with a tickle. She passed Lux's work shed and heard van doors shut. One slam, then another. She heard a man say something. She heard a woman giggle.

how can anyone laugh when he's dead?

She was sobbing now, weaving her way through old car parts, broken microwaves, mildewed couches stacked with TVs, vacuums, strollers, tires. Rainwater and leaves browned in a claw-foot tub, which she rounded at a run. They would never find her. They would never tell her what she didn't want to know. Deeper and deeper into junk, Sadie ran, panting, stumbling, bleeding, breathing,

come home, please, papa bear, just come home

LUX

Lux left the lady by the side of the road, but kept her mannequin. When he'd pressed the gun barrel to her temple, she seemed to seize with shock, to go cold and rigid as a corpse. It took her a quarter mile to pull over. It took a full five minutes to pull her from the vehicle. As Lux wheeled away, he watched her crumple in the rearview mirror.

Freed from his pocket, the kitten leapt toward the dash and slid onto the mannequin's lap, squinting its one eye at passing pines. The Buick drove smoother than the limo, had a better odor, too. Like leather and some sort of floral lotion. Like dried lilies and loneliness.

why do all old ladies smell the same?

Lux drove the ruts her car made on its way up. They swerved from side to side, feet deep in muck, at times veering straight toward the embankment. As if she'd been swigging gin behind the wheel, or intending to motor down the slope. In the passenger seat, pawing the mannequin's knee, the kitten turned another tight circle and curled around itself, purring. The sun was climbing the sky now, peeking through patches of cloud. Trees grew bare and spindly against a white horizon. Mud made thick, squishing sounds beneath the tires. Raindrops made pinegrass glisten.

Lux glanced at the figure, at the chisel of its jaw, the rigidity of its posture. He found facelessness unsettling, plastic silence unnerving. The fake man freaked him out. But it would be helpful, once he fetched Sadie, to appear as if they traveled with a third party. Were anyone to look for them, the mannequin would be a diversion, a distraction from their description: a gigantic, middle-aged male driving a miniature girl.

Lux looked at his pocket watch. Too much time had passed already, he had cut things too close.

we'll pack up and run today

He was sorry to have left the limo. He was sorry to have scared the lady. But these things were unavoidable. These things were out of his control. The limousine would be found, long after they were gone. The old woman would find her way back to town—with a story to tell and a renewed appreciation for every numbered breath.

To the mannequin, he said, "We should hurry. Sadie's probably awake. She's probably waiting." Lifting his boot from the brake, Lux let the weight of the Buick carry them down the hill. They continued, not talking.

When he'd told the woman to get out of the car, all she could say was, "Please." Over and over. Nothing but, "Please," tugging at Lux's sleeve, yanking at his sympathies. Her hands were veined and shaking, at once clinging for supplication, pressing for protection. The blood had drained from her face, even the round dots of rouge seemed to seep from her cheeks. One silver curl lost its whorl and lay limp on her forehead. He had to slide an arm under the lady's bony leg, just to remove her from the driver's seat. The crescent marks, made by her fingernails, still reddened his wrist.

she really thought I'd do it, she thought I'd shoot

Somehow, this realization hadn't registered during the ordeal. At the time, Lux was only thinking of Sadie. Of his baby, and how they would skip town, start over. Lock the past behind them and bolt. But careening now toward town, away from the woman, Lux felt sick. Rock-gutted with guilt. She might have heart failure on that winding, mountain road, he would never know. She might not be found for weeks. He passed the turn-off for town and kept driving.

As Lux accelerated down the highway, a mile from the junkyard driveway, a new terror overtook him. What if, during the night, Sadie had needed him? What if CPS beat him home? What if his girl was gone? Lux often thought of everyday activities as countdowns, routine actions as subtractions. How many more Sadie kisses would he get? How many whiskey-sips did he have left? How many shoe-ties, how many shits? Existence was shrinking imperceptibly—a bar of soap slipping away, thinning to a wafer, then to nothing at all. It was in these tiny deductions that death began. And now, in the midst of this daily extinction, they wanted to take his girl. To lose Sadie was to lose life. He swerved into the scrap yard at 60 mph.

The kitten clawed at the mannequin to keep from flying, as the Buick bounced over uneven, unhardened ground. Over mud and fresh tire tracks. Lux followed them to the house, careening to where several sets of footprints stopped at the porch stoop. He braked, compressing the pedal with such force, the car spun. The prints stamped several trips, to and from the house, every impression adult-size. Sadie must have been carried.

no, oh christ, no

Gearshift still in drive, Lux killed the engine, flung the door and his body into gray day. His soles sank. Sloppy soil made him slide. He moved in a slow motion dream-run, with the underwater progress of a nightmare. Before the porch, he slipped sideways, palm-planting into thick muck. It oozed between his fingers. Pawing, crawling, stumbling to a run, Lux took the stairs two at a time, at a bound that made planks squeak beneath his boots.

"Sadie?"

The screen door stood open at an angle. The wood door had been unlocked all night.

"Sadie!"

Lux lunged into the house, but the air inside told him it was empty. He ran the length of the hallway anyway, calling her name, streaming hot tears into his beard. Without sense or logic, Lux looked in places even Sadie couldn't squeeze: under the recliner, on closet shelves, behind curtains, in cupboards. He all but opened the silverware drawer.

Upstairs, the blankets on his bed were thrown back, the rocker cushion knocked to the floor. There was mud on the woven, oval rug. Someone had entered his room from outside. Someone had taken his Sadie.

be home, be home, sweetness, please

Yet every pore, open and knowing, told him she was gone. Sadie's presence displaced space as mass displaces water. When she was nowhere near, the atmosphere sank. Against time and reason, he hurried from room to room, looking everywhere for the little girl who was no longer there.

The staircase lurched, and a moment later, without remembering exiting, Lux stood in the scrap yard—swaying, seesawing. He felt nauseous. A soft rain fell. It misted the horizon, the piles of junk and pine trees walling the property. No matter which way he turned, the world wavered, shifted, inverted itself. Reeling in drizzle, Lux doubled over and puked: whiskey and bile and shame for what he'd done. For abandoning his kid, for losing his Sadie. For not leaving with her sooner. The sun couldn't come through the clouds. The gun was still in his pocket.

Lux touched the muzzle. His body had warmed the metal, and his fingernail flicked at the barrel. Then, as if whispered from an outside source, there came a thought—pressing, commanding, soundless.

the yard, search the scrap yard

Something made a quick flip in Lux's chest, the last vestige of hope which had lain latent, stored in blood and bone and hurt. He walked to the edge of the lot, his stride quickening beneath him, the sky swirling above. A crow flapped claps overhead, then drifted on invisible currents, cutting a V into clouds. Lux hadn't looked in their forts. Of course Sadie would have gone there.

of course

She would be in the hideaway they built the other day. She would be under cover, crouching on bare earth. In a corner, beneath BB gun holes—cold, and alone, and overjoyed to see him. Lux broke into a run, kicking a moldy dollhouse, scurrying a rat from the tiny dining room. It scampered past, hairless tail pulling a line through mud.

To anybody but Sadie and Lux, the fort would have blended unnoticed into the endless chaos of junk, which heaped, rusted, rotted, tangled, and piled, acre after acre. Between a six-foot pyramid of beer bottles and a mound of obsolete computer parts, their fortress concealed itself. This was the first place Sadie would choose to hide. Moving closer, Lux could sense she was inside. He could feel her. Sighing relief, he pushed open the door—a sandwich board that read, *Foot Long Hoagies: 2 for $5.25.* Its panels swung then broke from poorly soldered hinges, clapping together with a bang against soil.

He stood staring. In that instant, Lux's grief returned, redoubled. The enclosure was dim, Sadieless, speckled with light from the galaxy of BB gun stars. They shone constellations onto the ground, dots the child had connected with stick-lines in the dirt. Most were unrecognizable shapes, enigmatic and alien as crop circles. But both the Big and Little Dipper were discernible, crude trapezoids with angled handles. Against the wall, a tea party was set for two: plastic pot, plastic saucers with matching cups, mudcakes on a small, plastic platter. The pastries still held impressions of Sadie's fingerprints, tiny dints in dirt, dents where she'd molded mud and imagination into dainty bites.

Lux stayed there, stooped over in the small doorway, lower than he'd been a moment before. Scattered beside the tea set were three marbles: red, aquamarine, and umber. Wherever Sadie'd been taken, she was surely wishing they were in her pocket. If only to rub, between forefinger and thumb, for comfort. If only to remind her of Lux and love.

if only . . . the two saddest words ever

Turning from the empty hideaway, from any anticipation of seeing his kid again, he began to walk, lead-stepping into the scrap yard. Spring seemed to have retreated, to have arrived, then changed its mind.

He was done. Lux was stripped of all meaning and matter, pared bare. The gun made the right side of his pants sag. It was heavier than when first pocketed. No object had ever held more import, more loaded possibility and pointed significance.

Lux pressed deeper into the scrap yard, out of his mind lonesome. He passed the work shed where Sadie first learned to solder, where they welded their watchdog, Fox. He passed the rusted refrigerator where she'd curled on the center shelf to sleep. He passed heaps of tin cans, dunes of discarded buoys and netting, mounds of miscellaneous motor parts. These artifacts of human experience, the refuse of others, rolled like knolls across the junkyard, making landmarks in their shared landscape. His girl knew every bend of rebar, every disassembled and rusted appliance, every ream of electrical wire. His girl who was gone.

Below the oak, he stopped. A cool breeze blew, slanting rain. From the highway, a horn honked warning, amplifying as it approached and echoing away. Lux looked up. Branches stenciled geometric against sky—forms which begged to become symbols, yet remained meaningless in his mind. Metaphors seemed to demand some belief in a whole, some drive to find narrative. But Lux's world was shattered, no longer possible to piece together. Above him, wind wound new configurations with twigs, each as incomprehensible as the next.

In a final attempt to understand, to be understood, Lux stepped forward. Palm to trunk, he tried to sense the tree's pulse. This was something Sadie always did: *Papa Bear, I can feel its living . . . I feel its living in my fingers!*

Lux felt nothing but gnarled bark and the stick of sap. Nothing but the press of consciousness, and the weight of being. His head fell forward, hitting oak with a thonk. There was little left to do but take leave of a life already over. Bow out below twisted, leafless limbs.

just sit, sit the fuck down and submit

Turning, facing the lot, Lux pushed his back against bark, slid to a squat, settled on coiled roots and scattered rocks. His spine bowed perfectly into the curve of the trunk. All around him, wet earth held new life, growing green toward light. Eyes closed, wrists veined by fists, he sniffed at spring, thought of Sadie. Her lower lip-quiver as she expressed an idea. Her hand, patting softly at his flank fat when he felt sad, when Lux's past drowned out his present, when all that would soothe was her presence and she knew it. Her gray eyes and their otherworldliness when she woke, blinking into being. The child would be all right. She would remember how to live, how to move forward, how to forget. Lux had given her all he had, and now it was time to take.

which will be my very last gift

For one last time, Lux allowed himself to drift. He remembered Cal, twirling, whirling moon-eyed in a purple sundress, pointer finger curling him closer, *Come, Lux, come here*. He remembered her back to life: dappled by dogwood shade, laughing on the lawn, baby Sadie thrown over her shoulder. *Let's just be, Lux. Just us three, not so very complicated, huh?* He remembered Calista then, how bright light bloomed petals inside her irises. How her voice rose two octaves with any untruth. How she held off her own sleep to hold them—Sadie and Lux, daddy and baby—curling her body around theirs, folding them into one being. Then leaving them cold.

Beneath the tree, Lux floated. He was finished, through. Every blink of a lid, each twitch of a toe—they no longer belonged to him. He had abandoned himself as subject (with all its weight and wonder) and accepted himself as object (with all its blank and oblivion). Reaching again for the gun, he opened his pocket to metal and darkness. To lint and nothingness. Lux released the safety, cocked the trigger, lifted the barrel to his temple.

The impact, jarring against his skull, made Lux lurch under the oak. Death was immediate, intimate. It looked no different than life.

At his boots, a marble rolled. It was slow-moving, Mars-red.

He blinked, again and again, disbelieving the simple fact of his own seeing. The glass ball hit a root, making the uncorking sound of a champagne celebration. Before Lux could consider what hereafter he'd entered, another shot struck his head. Baffled, suddenly reverting to self-preservation, he balled his body, made a helmet of both hands.

soon, soon it will be over

There was a cracking then, high above him. Lux opened

his eyes. Stunned by sight, by any ability to experience, he watched a second marble roll. Its blue bumped his boot, ricocheted off a stone, then stopped by the rotting carcass of an acorn. Sprawled in mud, Lux flipped from his stomach, faced the sky, stared up.

Overhead, between boughs and his own disbelieving, a small palm waved. It dangled between twigs, wiggled familiar fingers. It signaled to him from the steel sculpture nest, wriggled a nail-bitten hello. Peering over rebar, Sadie's gray eyes held his, squinting a smile. She dropped another marble.

"Papa Bear, hi. Hi, Papa, I'm up here."

TEAL

Teal's grief was aging, and today it turned three. Anniversaries always struck her as arbitrary. Days of little significance, save for their correlation with some bygone moment of import. Dates of retrospect and regret. Annual observances which pushed the present back toward the past, imposed recall, obligated memory. This particular morning—this 11:40 in the Blue Moon Motel, in bleached light and broken sleep—mattered no more than any other. No more than every near-noon that had passed unnoticed before.

Moaning, Teal rolled on the mattress, pulled the quilt over her head. Its fabric smelled of must, cigarette butts, the dime store musk she dabbed behind her ears. It was tattered and dirty and darkened the window's glow—obliterated clean, April light. Teal's dad had loved spring, lived for the season. He would rise early, when morning still had that rich earth smell of something about to be. He would dress in the dim to walk down dawn streets, to see the world wake with newness.

Teal repositioned onto her side, thought about the day

he died—the day that was exactly three years past and now unfolding. Again. She thought about his face, fixed and yellow against the pillow. She thought about how his skin felt, cool and smooth as glass to touch. About how, in that instant, the landscape went flat and blank. Soon thereafter, she left home's warm enclosure. Where she felt pointless and poisonous as an appendix.

Teal viewed her life with a sense of inevitability, like a myth, or a story moral. Events happened because they had to. Because every iron and welded link led, on some chain of causality, to their necessity. Decisions were predestined, set off by previous effects. Actions were reactions, choices were consequences. She was thus shackled, freed from responsibility. Bound only to unfettered experience, to emotion outside of her control. Today, Teal would stay in bed.

Theo can fend for himself

The old man had been out of sorts lately, ever since Ferrah flapped away. Since Lux started visiting, and Teal started loving. Last Tuesday, she caught Theo listening at her door—pale and trembling in terrycloth. When she stepped outside, he had all but fallen onto her liver-colored carpet.

"Oh, just 'bout to knock," he said, holding out a bowl of grapes. Every skin had been peeled.

"Oh, just 'bout to leave."

Theo's face collapsed like an accordion. They never discussed Lux. But Teal knew her neighbor knew: about the late nights, about the rusted limo parked out front, about the man who would spread her legs like a blackjack hand, like a fool hitting on twenty. Often, when the bedsprings sang and Lux cried out, she would urge their writhing toward the armchair, press a palm over his open mouth. It was essential to protect Theo, best she could. All that ever mattered to the old man had disappeared into cloud, diminished into dust—his parrot, his daughter. And now Teal was spending less and less time caring for him. Theo's longing for her had no end. There would be no bottom to his loss.

In a t-shirt and panties, Teal stretched against the sheets, remembering the first time she saw Lux. He'd been walking the long, white shore, calling after a child who darted through driftwood like an intoxicated pixie. From a park bench, she watched him wander by the water, pink ice cream dripping down his sleeve.

When they spoke, weeks later in O'Blivion's, Teal knew he would love her. She could always sense it, the moment she met a soon-to-be-mate. Like an animal, she could smell it. Something inside of her perked, crouched, set stance for stalk or surrender. Positioned for seduction or submission. Before she learned the names of lovers, she could feel their fucking. Across a room, she could feel fingers across her forehead. Down a hall, she could feel lips down her flank. Over barroom chatter, she could feel hands over her chest. These intuitions of intimacy didn't actualize the event, didn't precipitate the sex. They were, rather, sixth-sensory previews. Teasers, like movie trailers or appetizers.

The curtains weren't drawn all the way, and a slat of bright slanted toward the bed. She stared at the inch-width of light, wishing night would hurry up and blacken day. Weather never minded her mood. Below a spackled ceiling and unwashed covers, Teal began to sob. For her father, who had suffered. For Theo, who had withered inside. For herself, and the balloon she'd let go of when she was five. For every hope that had floated away, bobbing skyward to become a dot and pop.

Just as Teal teared through the top sheet, just as her blubbering silenced itself into the open-mouthed, closed-eyed cry that wracks drunks and toddlers alike, there was a pounding on the door. A thudding that was not Theo's secret knock, not his series of staccato strikes followed by a kick.

who the fuck

The do-not-disturb sign dangled from the knob. Save for the thin strip of sun, the curtains were drawn, tacky-striped and tight against morning. Someone had the wrong room. Teal would wait it out. She hunkered under the covers, willing away the afternoon intrusion. Nobody but the old man and the motel maid knew where she lived. Nobody but—

Lux

Teal threw back blankets, wiped frantically at mascara that ran black rivulets down her cheeks, charcoal-staining her pillowcase. She hurried from the bed to the door, then back to the bed again. She tugged at her shirt, tried to stretch its cotton to cover bare skin. She grabbed a pair of sweats from the floor.

"Okay. All right, just a sec."

The thumps came again. Lux's knock was as distinctive as his voice: abrupt, insistent, strident. His every movement asserted identity, announced individuality: glances in public were an imprint, bootprints in sand a signature. The motel door rattled on its hinges, the chain lock shook its links.

Now Teal had no doubt who stood, waiting and wanting, outside. She knew who would be leaning, slant-smiled and hulking in the doorjamb. Huge and hoping in spring sun. Pulling at her drawstring with one hand, the knob with the other, Teal opened to Lux and bright.

No matter how often she saw him, his size always startled her. A behemoth bulk molded for another world, a world of higher ceilings, reinforced and ample armchairs, shoehorns like elephant ears, bathtubs the size of lap pools. Across his jaw, hair grew thatched and patchy. Ruddy and glowing where sun hit, where it lit whisker-tips. Lux tilted his head, shifted his stance, mute and staring.

Teal lowered her eyes, twirled her hair, quiet and blinking.

Behind him, in the parking lot, raindrops dried on asphalt. Behind her, in the motel room, teardrops dried on cheap sheets. A car honked and a faucet dripped. A breeze blew and a fan droned. Separating them was silence and two decades.

"You look a mess," Lux said.

"I am a mess," said Teal. She could feel the smear of makeup around her eyes, the dried slime of sleep caked around her mouth, crusting her words.

While not naturally self-conscious, her job had instilled a certain vanity, an inability to escape the awareness of I-ness. Wherever she walked, however she talked, Teal saw herself from the outside. Through strip-club lights and other people's eyes. Nights on stage had done this to her. Nights of cigar smoke and stolen gropes, when she stepped from dress to skin, from subject to object. In pancake makeup and five-inch heels, Teal cherished these hours of performance and detachment—these parades of playacting and escape. Pirouetting the pole, she felt like a nude marionette, like her movements were string-controlled and no longer her own. As if she needed only to drift and to dream.

But in the doorway, in streaking eyeliner and grief, Teal felt more naked than she did on stage. She felt displayed, flayed. Unadorned and exposed as herself. Shifting from one bare foot to the other, Teal looked away.

Lux shuffled his boots, cleared his throat. "I can only stay for a bit . . . Sadie's waiting." He turned toward the parking lot. He nodded toward the lone car, a yacht-size Buick, his gaze all the while holding her askance. "Is everything, um—is there anything . . . I brought you something." From his pocket, Lux pulled a foil package.

"Oooh." Teal's voice rose through the vowel, drawling it long. She crossed both arms over her breasts, which were braless beneath the thin shirt. She didn't reach for the gift.

"Just something Sadie n' I picked up. Just something we, ah, we picked out. It was her idea, really. Not mine."

"Did the limo break down? Whose car you driving?" Behind Lux, a silver Le Sabre sat sighing exhaust out its tailpipe.

He glanced at the Buick, then back at his offering, pushing the pouch closer to her folded arms.

"Who's that there with Sadie?" In the passenger seat, a bald man sat perfectly still.

"Here. Cracker Jacks," he said, shrugging apology. "Sorry. It's just the inside part. No box, 'cause my kid wanted to keep it. Wanted the prize, too, but I told her that was for you. I told her that's what gifting means. Always to give away the good part."

"Oh," she said again. Behind Lux, in the Buick's backseat, the child's face was slack above a picture book. Whoever was with her did not move. Teal stared at the girl. Then again at the adult, who was seatbelted and bolt–straight up front. "Does your—does she want to come in, or something?"

"Sadie? Nah," Lux shook loose, unshaven skin. "Nope, she's happy."

"Really?"

"Plenty."

"Whose car is that?"

"Borrowing it. So, I wanted to tell you. . ." His eyes widened, darted. "Can we—can we go in for a second, can we step inside," he asked, suddenly formal. His gigantic head tilted, heavy–maned as a lion's, toward her room. "May I?"

"What?" Teal didn't step aside. She was still staring at the unfamiliar vehicle, at the glint of the pane, the tiny girl bent over her book.

"Is that man a—Lux, why is there . . . Do you have a goddamn mannequin in there?"

He nodded toward her room. "Can we go inside, Teal? Please?"

LUX & SADIE

The rain finally stopped, but Lux drove with the wipers flailing wild. Beating back and forth, the blades screeched against the windshield, lifted the little hairs on Sadie's arms. Bugs smeared guts across the glass. Dirt streaked, blurring the whole world. Sadie missed home while road-grime rainbowed beneath the wipers.

Lux said the limo got lost, but they had a brand new Buick. It came with a mannequin, a kitten, and a dead flower smell. The mannequin was silent and plastic. The kitten was missing an eye and mewing. The smell was making Sadie sick. She sat in the backseat, staring at Lux, at his profile in twilight, his eyes in the rearview mirror—veined pink and squinting, fast-blinking at every car that passed. As they neared town, he sighed and the Buick felt smaller around her.

why're you worried, papa bear?

———

Lux coughed, tugged at his beard.

A scudding sky was closing in, blackening fast. The car splashed past mile marker 4. Then came the grade school—with its crosswalk, hopscotch, geodesic jungle gym—and mile marker 3. Then the nursing home, mile marker 2. In the rearview mirror, Sadie stared straight ahead, motionless. Her hands formed fists by her hips, as if, at any second, she might need to counter a punch. On the right side of the road, Ribs 'n' Racks strip club pulsed a strobe and some swanky, take-it-off tune. Along the building's west wall, a line of men stood smoking, backs pressed to brick.

Teal, she's probably in there

Lux watched the club recede, the road unwind behind, the confusion contort Sadie's expression. Her head had fallen back and watchful, her smile had fallen slack. Leaving the lot, she'd been chipper and fluttery, fairly flying, mistaking his anxiety for excitement. Now the kid sat still. Alert and creepy-quiet.

she knows

He was often stunned, unsettled even, by Sadie's intuition—by her ability to notice the slightest shift in his affective stance. She began to lose interest in the kitty, letting it leap from her lap to explore the underside of the dash, the pedals Lux pumped up and down with his unlaced boot.

Back at the scrap yard, the girl had tied a length of twine into a limp leash, looping it over the kitten's misshapen face. The string tangled now, twisting around the gearshift and Lux's ankle. Around the cup-holder and gas pedal. As he took a hairpin at high-speed, the critter skittered beneath the brake and began to purr with the whirr of the engine. Its rat tail stuck out, bright white in the dim. Lux kicked at the cat.

"Shit, gonna get us killed." His steel toe pushed into fur, and the kitten squeaked a piccolo note. "Little mutant."

"Come'ere, Mutan'," Sadie called absently, cluck-clucking her tongue. But the kitty jumped over the center console, began to muzzle-nuzzle the mannequin's shin.

"Ha. That what you're gonna name it? Mutant?"

She didn't answer.

Lux kneaded a neck knot and glanced again at the girl. She was framed by the rearview mirror, slouched against the car door, looking scared and scarred.

"I know a game, Sweetie, a real fun one. Wanna play?"

———

He said something she didn't hear. Something to make everything all right, even though it wasn't. Even though it never would be again. She was unsure where they were driving, or why the beat of Lux's words made her heart drum double-time. He hunched over the wheel while the landscape—purple hills, russet fields, slate sky—slipped on all sides by. His posture looked pained, slumped, a hunkering defense against Sadie's silence and the sliding sun. Soon, it would be dark. Soon, there would be only road ahead. Above, only a vast, blank black where night clouds blotted out stars.

They'd packed up fast, duffle-stuffing items Lux deemed needed. For what, Sadie didn't know. With a sinking, quicksand feeling, she scanned the supplies by her sneakers: cans of Spam, matches, snack-size Cheetos, two toy trucks she'd begged to bring along from the scrap yard.

Less from appetite, more from agitation, she pulled the

Cheetos out from under a box of bullets. The foil crinkled with fire crackles, like wood sparking and snapping. This made Lux look away from the road, meet her stare in the mirror. Sadie crunched, munching loud and rude. Chewing and swallowing calmed her, allowed her to fall into a comfy stupor. To feel at home inside herself.

By and by, the strange car and the long day faded away, until there was only the chomp-chomp of Cheetos between her teeth, the opening and closing of her mouth. But when the bag was empty, the anxiety returned in full. Now the seatbelt was tighter, the atmosphere thicker. She pressed a palm to the window. An orange print waved back, stuck to the glass.

Sadie sucked florescent cheese from her fingertips. "Why can't we just camp at home, though? Like we always do, Papa? Why'd we have to drag the tarp n' stuff out here?"

Lux accelerated, said nothing. His face was embossed by shade, cribbled with pockmarks. Sometime, when she wasn't looking, he had grown very old.

Sadie sniffed, "Besides, the ground's wet. Mud's every-place."

On both sides of the road, dead fields waved in the wind. She knew, if Lux would only slow down, that a whispering sound would surround them.

dry stalks talk to us

They passed a cow byre, a baler, a motorbike course where townie boys crushed Coors cans on weekends, loud-revving around and around over dirt mounds. Barns blurred by. Empty acreage, brown ponds, pastures with ponies standing shag-haired and still.

"Will the plastic man have his own sleeping bag, or be in one of ours?"

Lux let out a short chortle. A half laugh, or a groan. Sweat stippled his stubble. "So the game, Sweets, it goes like this—"

Something in the mirror stopped him. Behind the Buick, emergency lights ignited night, blazing crimson over the dashboard, the back of the mannequin's bald head, the fear on Lux's face.

"Cops," he breathed. "Get the fuck down." Lux mouthed her name, followed by three words which were swallowed by approaching wails.

"What?"

"Down! Now!"

"Why?"

As Sadie twisted around to see, the police car flared red-blue-red, tailgated, and changed into an ambulance. It veered toward the passing lane, flashed her blind, then sirened out of sight.

"Not cops, Papa Bear."

Lux exhaled. The kitten repositioned on the mannequin's lap. They drove a while, or a mile.

"So, anyway," he continued, looking haggard, "it's a hiding game I was telling you about. When a car comes, any car, duck real quick. Try and hit the deck before they see you, 'kay?"

Sadie played for a bit, but quit when she realized there was no way to win. They were far from anything familiar, far from the only town she'd known—where fields shrank to lawns, farmhouses became manufactured homes, spruce trees switched to street signs. Where the lake shallowed toward shore, docks dotted the waterline like lily pads, and Lux loved her for always. His neck looked damp, clammy-cold. A vein protruded on his temple. He stopped talking altogether.

———

Lux ran out of words.

much farther, and we'll be out of gas

Now he and Sadie would run, toward freedom to be and a new kind of together. A hundred miles down the highway, they would ditch the Buick with its plastic passenger. They would bivouac in the dense forests surrounding Cody, then dump their stuff and thumb the four-hour ride to the city. Over mountains and mounting paranoia, against thunder skies and all odds.

we'll last a month, at most

Beyond a pasture of sleepy cows and rusted plows, the lake came back into view. Rippling shoreward, shifting reflections. The surface frilled, ruffling taffeta. In that moment, Lux remembered Sadie's mother, wavering forever in his mind, hazing forever from Sadie's recollection. He shivered and thought of Cal, burning. Her body, its beauty marks, stretch marks, track marks. The fingers he loved so much, long and nail-nibbled, almost alienesque. The ends of her hair, split-frayed and tangled. The curve of her thigh, the curl of her smile. All reduced to dust. All Ziploc'd, scattered into the lake to swirl then sink.

Lux could make no sense of this. Of one human being cupped in another's palm, tossed like a handful of sand to sift down and down through ancient glacier water. For such experiences, there were no words. Only sappy quotations, sad approximations.

He imagined the lake floor, 1400 feet below boat wakes and breath. A secret terrain, lightless and silent. A landscape of sunken vessels, abyssal hills, prehistoric fish with human faces. At what depth did Cal finally settle? On what sandstone shelf, on what binnacled—now barnacled—bow? Or was she as restless in death as she had been in life? Perhaps particles of her person still swirled, riding rudderless and lost on moon tides. Lux sighed again. Leaving Cody County, they were leaving Calista—and Sadie didn't even realize it.

"Papa?"

He wiped the wet from his face, cleared his throat. "We should try to find our constellations tonight, Baby . . . if it clears up."

"Uh, huh."

"Was that a *yay*, or a *nay*?"

The kitten squeaked. The child stayed quiet, watching day die outside her window.

Lux thought of Teal, all alone in the motel. By now, she would be smudging on blush, slicking back black strands before work. The eyeliner she always did first: cross-legged and topless on the bathroom counter, in panties and a hurry. Lux loved how the girl's vertebrae lengthened when she leaned toward the mirror, her lids lowering as if for a kiss. How charcoal smoked around her eyes, making umber irises smolder at the center like embers. Teal would be missed, though not unbearably.

"Wanna make a fire tonight, Baby?

As Lux was leaving the motel, he'd felt a spine-tingle of sentimentality. A shiver which began in his bones, quivered his capillaries, shuddered the holding chambers of his heart. Teal had changed him. She had brought Lux back to Before—to life before body aches and love-breaks. Before hollowing loss and howling-at-the-moon sorrow.

Teal had revived him, simplified him, reminded him of the world before it wobbled off-axis. Before it whirled forever out of control. When connections were uncomplicated, intimacy uninhibited. The girl animalized desire, returned lust to a state of instinct and exigency. To a mauling, clawing, mounting must-have. They coupled whenever, wherever they could. By lamplight or streetlight. In alleyways, on bathmats, behind do-not-disturb signs. Under spring rain or infinite specks of stars. It was baying, biting sex—ferocious, rapacious. Sex before it became domesticated, housetrained as a cocker spaniel.

Lux glanced at the passenger seat. At this point, even the mannequin looked exhausted. He, too, was far from home. Two hours earlier, while Sadie waited in the Buick, Lux had tried to memorize Teal. Her black hair spilling like ink over her body; her lashes casting palmette shadows below her eyes; her face shifting shape as Lux lied. He'd reclined against the sheets and made up a story. A story about Sadie. About the kid's wish to travel outside Cody County, and their ensuing camping trip.

"It'll just be for a few days. Three . . . maybe four."

Teal's quilt had smelled of Pall Malls lit late-night. Of insomniac smoke, and some cheap perfume for teenagers. Mascara streaked her cheeks, her pillowcase where she'd been sobbing. About what, Lux could only guess. Monthly mood-swings? Mistreatment at the strip club? That creep next door with a birdcage and a shit-brown bathrobe? He didn't know, nor did he care to ask. When it came to the woes of women, Lux learned long ago never to inquire.

Beside the bed, a clock had tocked their last seconds together. The window was pushed open, the curtain pulled closed. He'd dressed quickly, saying that Sadie was ready to hit the road. As Lux lied and lied, Teal rolled from the mattress to pose nude and contrapposto by the mini-fridge. She was sulky, sweaty, still wearing socks. Her waist tapered near the navel, rounding downward toward a soft-shaded triangle. Around her neck was a chain, dangling some sort of amulet. The charm flashed between her breasts. For eyes, the girl had two circles of shade. From their depths, she seemed to be studying Lux's mouth, his lips moving around untruths.

Evening was descending now, dusking indigo. Twilight stretched, submerging the landscape into lush shadow.

"D'you know, Sweetie, that some people call this time of night 'owl light?'"

Sadie squirmed, kicked the mannequin's seat, planted another cheese print on the window.

Lux felt the impulse to grab the girl by her scruff.

"Why?"

———

"Why, what?" His voice sounded wooden, splintered.

"Why's it for owls?"

"'Cause this is the kind of light owls love, the kind they

156

feel free flying in."

The Buick rocked like a rowboat, making Sadie sick to her stomach. But Lux always felt better when chatting, so again she asked, "Why?"

He cracked his back, then his neck. "'Cause it's dim, and everything feels magic and new in the dark. Alive and creepy-crawly under the moon. Owls love that. And also because no one else can see 'em."

"Sorta like us, like how you said we're night owls?"

Lux winced a grin. "Yeah. Yeah, sure. I guess it's the same."

The sky was made of papier-mâché; the lake was made of sheet metal. Against a dry windshield, the wipers continued to thrash. Lux didn't notice. The car began its climb, winding out of the valley and away from Cody County. He sped hard toward the hill, leaning into the incline as if his weight might tip them up and over the slope. They could still see the water. They probably always would. Below, it was serpentine and still—like a river at rest. It gleamed green around the shoreline, glinted metallic at the center. It held minnows, and memories, and someone Sadie could barely recall. Someone she missed more than anything.

Staring down, watching the lake sparkle and shrink, Sadie knew, suddenly, what Lux would not say. Calista was gone. Forever-gone. Can't-come-back gone. The kind of gone that morphs a person into a photograph, a lover into a moan, a mother into a storybook chapter read less and less often before bed.

Miles behind them, the water became a puddle, what remains after April rains. A mirror that wrinkled, rippled, refused to stay the same. In its silver, Sadie saw Calista. Swimming toward the surface, pressing both palms to the underside of the glass—smiling.

———

Lux's eyes itched, his temples ached. The sooner the Buick was off the road, the better. Cresting the hill, he didn't look back—at the lake, at Calista. *66 mph . . . 71 mph.* Theirs had been a sharp-toothed love. *78 mph . . . 83 mph.* A love that was serrated, liable to slice him in two. *90 mph.* And indeed it had.

"A little longer, Sadie. Just a bit farther, Baby."

"But what'll Mutan' eat, what'll he get for his camping dinner?"

"Same as what we're gonna enjoy. Spam 'n Cheetos. Got us some Ho-Hos, too. Anyway, what makes you so sure it's a boy cat?"

"Easy-peasy. He's got that. . ." she fumbled for the word, then for one of the toy trucks by her foot. "He's got that boy look in his eyes—in his, um . . . eye."

"You can tell, huh?"

Sadie squirmed against the seat. She rolled the truck back and forth over her safety belt, making vroom-vroom sounds. The kitty started snoring, pink nose pressed to the crease of the mannequin's collar.

we'll ditch both of 'em, once off the highway

The plastic man would be found with the Buick, maybe even returned to the old lady—or to whatever mall he called home. As for the cat, Lux wasn't so sure. A familiar guilt snaked up his spine. He had no provisions for the kitten, no patience for the mewing, for all the scurrying and scratching and peeing. He'd only pocketed the little goblin to make Sadie smile.

And smile she had. On the porch, beneath gabled eaves and new leaves, she created a nest for the beast: a butter dish with a napkin for a blanket. But the two shared just a few hours in the junkyard, before they were Buicked away. All the furry bastard left behind was a cat comb (clumped with fluff), and a cardboard box (clumped with petrified shit). Kittylittered rolls that reminded Lux of Almond Rocas.

Sadie unbuckled, stretched across the console to pet the cat. Humming softly, she stroked its deformed features, its folds of excess face and nictitating membrane. A tiny tongue licked back. Lux stared, overwhelmed by revulsion and affection.

"Honey, uh . . . Sadie, Sweetie, no. Nu'uh. Buckle up. Who knows where that snout's been. How 'bout we don't touch Mutant's, um, eye area. Okay? Buckle back up, Hon."

With her fingernail, she continued to tickle wrinkled skin. Sadie's pinkie was the same size as the kitty's paw pad.

"I think Mutan's real pretty. All that white fur around his face. And look how his nose moves when he's happy."

Sadie was feeling better, Lux could tell.

———

Lux was relaxing a little, Sadie could tell. He steered with only one hand now, its knuckles no longer talons around the wheel. From the scraggles of his beard came a tinny whistle: a music box tune Sadie recognized. A string of sixteenth notes scaling up and up, reminding her of a spindly iron staircase, corkscrewing skyward. The box sat on a shelf in their thrift store. Customers often creaked open the case, heard its song—a creepy trebling—and quickly closed the lid. But Lux's tune soothed Sadie, smoothed away her worry with its melody. She sat back in her seat to listen and the Buick hummed along, droning low accompaniment.

Out the window, mountains and miles flew by. Orchards, vineyards, train yards with boxcars. Lux's song whistled on, and the rain began again. First in pitter-patter drizzle, then in whopping drops that walloped the hood, threatened to dent the aluminum roof. Sadie was suddenly very sleepy. Her limbs were limp, her eyelids heavy as barbells. She slumped against the door, let dusk take her.

———

Beneath water splashing, wipers thrashing, and Lux whistling, there was another noise. A rasping with its own rhythm. Lux stopped his song, cocked his head, angled his mirror. In the backseat, Sadie had fallen asleep. A scratchy, dry-leaf sound scraped from her open mouth. A sound reminiscent of a different season, when oaks dropped orange and gold to crackle underfoot, when the earth sprang alive with decay.

But spring was here now. It was bursting rebirth, scenting this April night with the promise of green. Out in the dark, in the rain, rootlets reached toward newness. Vines climbed, robins huddled together, and hawk moths shook off cocoons. Before long, Sadie would breathe easier, freer. Lux wanted nothing more than to turn in his seat and watch the girl sleep. To stroke her hand, say her name. It was all he had left. But rain hammered, and the road whiplashed curves. Yellow lane-lines sped at them, head-on.

soon, need to pull over soon

His vision bleared, and his high beams shafted bright into black. All the world was shadow and water, silhouette and wet. The sky was pouring, bucketing, but Lux felt drained—dog-tired and ready to drop. They had to get off the highway. He skidded into turns, muscles clenched tight. He accelerated into straight-aways, eyes scared wide. The Buick seemed to be speeding through a carwash, or surfing the underside of a wave. Lux squinted, slowed, swerved off the road.

———

Sadie woke to weightlessness. To languagelessness, and Lux lifting her from the seat. He held her close, cooing. He hugged her hard, saying sweet things she couldn't understand. Then she was floating through night air, smelling mud mixed with whiskey. Rain mixed with fear. Lux's chest was huge and heaving against her face.

"Papa?"

For a few steps, he baby-cradled Sadie. He cupped her head, rocked her body from side to side, before setting her down in knee-high weeds. She stood, reeling. Muck sucked at her sneakers. She sank to the ankle. Wind wound hair around her throat, over her eyes, while drops battered cold and sharp.

She glanced back to look for the Buick.

It was muted in monochrome, shadowed in a shallow marsh. Already, reeds seemed to surround the car, to sprout in tall tufts by the tires. Vines appeared to twine over the hubcaps, grow under the grills, thread through the fenders. Sadie imagined the Buick as long-abandoned, as one of the ghost cars on their junk lot. Stripped skeletal, rotting from the inside, with rats gnawing the upholstery and rust corroding the paint. She couldn't see the mannequin, but she knew he was there—waiting, wondering when they'd return.

Lux grabbed her hand. "C'mon."

"But the kitty!" Panic seized Sadie. "What about Mutan'?"

"The cat ran ahead. Let's go, huh? Let's follow." He began to walk, trudging through sludge. Lux muttered something else, but his words sank, drowned in the downpour.

———

"We'll be all right, Sweets, you'll see." The sentence calmed him, even though he didn't believe it. Even though Sadie didn't hear it. Just as, a few minutes before, she hadn't heard Lux shooing the kitten from the Buick.

While Sadie slept, Lux had plucked Mutant off the mannequin's lap, opened the car door, and set the cat gently on mud. He'd done his best to hiss, to whisper the creature away—*Get on now, go*—all the while remembering his own father with Fox.

"We're close, Sadie, keep going. Almost there, Lovey."

The kid stubbed her toe on a stone and whimpered. A stalactite of snot hung from one nostril. Her blonde was plastered black against her face. Lux was all but dragging the girl, urging her toward the woods and its bower shelter. Toward the border of the forest, only fifty yards off.

Thunder cracked, rain sharded, and the moon looked broken. Sadie stumbled to keep stride beside Lux. Every step stuck deeper. Her slicker was unzipped, her whole body in shivers. But she knew the cat was up ahead, counting on her to continue. So she did. Until one sneaker stayed fixed to its print, while her sock kept walking.

"Papa Bear!" she screamed, pulling her hand from his, hollering over wind and pounding water. "Papa, my foot!"

He turned. The duffle bag rounded from his back, making Lux look like an enormous tortoise. Under one arm he carried the tarp, bungeed around two sleeping sacks. In the other hand, he beamed a flashlight this way and that. Top heavy, bending bit by bit, Lux helped Sadie back into her shoe. Moonlight filigreed through trees, providing just enough bright for Sadie to see conifer outlines, outcrops of rock. Lux's face looked twisted, burled. She took his hand again.

Together, they slogged on.

Yard after yard, bushes thickened. The ground was harder to tread now, foliated by high ferns, duff, layer upon layer of leaves. Moss hammocked from branches. A rich, mushroomy smell wafted, wet and heavy. Above, tree limbs tunneled where pine needles thatched. Sadie and Lux continued, where crickets leapt and thickets closed around them. Ahead, a line of trunks grew straight and thick, columned in an orderly row. The earth below looked dry underneath, the surrounding dark strangely welcoming.

bet that's where Mutan' went

Approaching the grove, tromping brave beside her papa, Sadie felt suddenly safe. The trees knew how to endure, how to stay rooted together.

She yanked at Lux's jacket. "That the forest?"

"Yup . . . well, the start of it, anyway. This is just the beginning." His boots led the way, stomped a new path through night.

Sadie didn't let go of Lux's hand until they reached the edge of the woods. Until her eyes got used to the dark.